SUMMER SESSION

A NOVEL

SUMMER SESSION

Summer Session is a work of Fiction. All people, places, events
and characters are created solely in the mind of the author.

This book is dedicated to my best friend Tony, the Extra P, who is fighting a never ending war.
Sorry you missed the best years of our lives.

PROLOGUE

QUINTIN BENNET

GRANDMASTER RENAISSANCE

"School never taught me how to succeed in life, just the institutional way of being an ideal American." - Aquanza Cadogan

The plan was to wait until she turned out the lights. We could hear the door shut down the hall, which signaled it was time to spring our plan into action. Quincy, already dressed from the waist down, jumped out of bed and began searching for the rest of his outfit. His generation liked their clothes snug, so the mohawk on his head made him look more like an ambitious rocker than a connoisseur of Hip Hop. I placed my Yankee fitted down just below my brim and picked up my dominos - ready to get it in. Conscious of exactly which boards in our old two-story brownstone would sound an alarm we quietly tip-toed down the hallway and quickly descended the stairs to meet Spelling. This nightly routine was much easier since our old man was overseas finishing his last military tour. He believed fighting for our country would lighten the burdens of his sins, make right all his juvenile wrongs. In some strange way his big Veterans check after retirement would be his first legal investment. The real problem was missing his two boys growing into young men.

Tonight we were headed to Club Memo, a popular club in the heart of Manhattan. Memo was the only place to be seen and earn teenage notoriety. The city labeled it the "Clash of the Boroughs," the biggest domino competition this side of the tri-state, and the Brooklyn champ Clean Slate and I were the headliners.

Queens was quiet after midnight, so we headed underground where man-made tunnels would help us emerge in the manufactured center of entertainment. Spelling was already waiting at the subway entrance as planned, wearing my favorite outfit for good luck.

"I thought ya'll wasn't coming anymore."

"You know how mom's is," I responded, leaning in for a kiss.

"We're going to be late lovebirds," Quincy shouted, hearing the screech of subway cars approaching the platform.

We all sprinted down the stairs laughing, racing to beat those automatic doors from ruining our evening. The sudden jerk of the train signaled our journey into the city.

Who am I?
I am New York's Finest...
I am Quintin Bennet.

MARQUEL HOWARD

BODY LANGUAGE

"If you don't design your own life plan, chances are you'll fall into someone else's." – Jim Rohn

Membership for this exclusive business was word-of-mouth only. The monthly dues, signing fees and service charges were unusually high and catered only to the wealthiest of clientele. Their money paid for the soft lighting and exotic music filling the small lounge. The receptionist informed me that my appointment book was filled today, which meant I'd be rushing to pick my son up again after my last client. My part-time job, which started as a way to make some extra cash, had blossomed into the largest all-male massage parlor in the South. Desire, our no-nonsense boss, ensured our high-end clientele and service went way beyond the norm to please our diverse all-female market.

> "Mrs. Crenshaw, back again so soon?" Denim asked, ushering her into his room and closing the door behind them.

Mrs. Crenshaw was the top art connoisseur in the Atlanta area, with four art museums that catapulted her into the "A-list" of the city's elite. Her second visit to Body Language this week could only mean Mr. Crenshaw was traveling on business again, and her cold, lonely nights needed some warmth. The next two clients were new to Body Language. The busty Caucasian followed The Mayor into his room while the hard-body Latina followed Zae' into his. I stood patiently in the hallway as a shy sista peeked around the corner.

> "Don't be nervous, I'm Young Denzel and welcome to Body Language," I stated closing the door behind us.

She smiled and without saying a word dropped her robe. Naked bodies were common in my profession but her anatomy was breathtaking. If skin was the largest pleasure organ then she was a walking billboard of satisfaction.

Too bad I was married, with a three-year-old tearing up my on-campus housing, and was trying to remain faithful in the epicenter of sex...

Who am I?
I am Young Denzel...
I am Marquel Howard.

HARLEM BEST

LITTLE DREAD

"If money doesn't change you, you're obviously not making enough." - Unknown

The freedom was in the riddim, the expression of the lyrics. Dancehall was to Reggae what Hip Hop music had become to urban youth. Defiant, crude and unpredictable, dancehall music was young Caribbean youth. The sexual gestures in the movements, the sheer power and truth behind the lyrics were far removed from the gentle non-violent approach of our elders. For these reasons alone dancehall music had spread its roots in major markets such as Asia and Europe and blossomed into flourishing art forms that stretched farther than the shores of the tiny island it originated from.

I sat outside my parents' tiny villa enjoying the unique taste of coconut water and sugar cane. Westmoreland Parish was always buzzing with tourists lured by the white-sandy beaches and clear blue waters of Negril. My mother made a living working at one of the many all-inclusive resorts along the beach by day and in her jerk chicken shop by night. My father was too busy pursuing his dream of becoming a musician and his passion had him playing the cruise-line circuit seven months of the year. The mellow sounds of Freddy McGregor flowed throughout the house as a crisp breeze from the ocean filled the island.

A smooth seven-series BMW pulled up alongside my mother's breadfruit tree and the words that shaped who I'd become were projected from the inside:

"Hey, Little Dread! Feel like making some money?"

I ran over to the car to meet Legacy, a Royal Jamaican/Indian drug lord that ran the parish.

"Sure!" I replied, causing him to break out in laugher.

"You don't even know what you have to do, and you're down for the cause Little Dread? I admire that."

"So what do I have to do?"

"Two cruise ships will be docking tomorrow around one. I've got two guys waiting for these packages," he said, flashing me two boxes.

"I need you to take these to them, no questions asked."

"That's it?"

"Yea, that's it, Little Dread. You do this for me and I'll give you this," he said, flashing an American $100 bill.

My eyes lit up, since American dollars were extremely valuable on the island. There was no telling how many things I could buy with that money.

"I'll be back around this time tomorrow to give you your money if everything goes well," Legacy stated handing me the two boxes.

At noon the next day, I walked a few miles with the two boxes hidden neatly in a backpack. I met Network and Mandatory, two of Legacy's foot soldiers who led me into a small room above a liquor store. I watched as they broke open the boxes to reveal pounds of marijuana.

"Good work Little Dread," Network announced, rubbing my tiny locks and showing me the exit. We'll make sure to tell Legacy you did a good job."

I would later come to realize that young kids with backpacks near cruise ships were far less suspicious than Legacy and his boys fishing around. That measly $100 dollars I made would later equate to millions for Legacy and his team.

The next day, as promised, Legacy showed up with my $100 bill and another proposition.

"Take a ride with me, Little Dread," he demanded, and just like that we were off. I became "Little Dread," Legacy's young protégé.

Over the next few months I would make thousands of American $100 bills. I would meet drug lords from every parish in Jamaica and eventually visit the fields that manufactured our product deep in the jungles.

Who Am I?
I am a true Rude Bwoy...
I am Harlem Best.

CAESAR GIBSON

DEADSTOCK

"What you are as a person is far more important than who you are as a basketball player." - John Wooden

Basketball, sneakers, graffiti and women – those were my four essential vitamins I consumed daily. My biggest problem was I couldn't keep them in that order. My art class was filled with the scent of expensive acrylic paint and untamed creativity. I was familiar with the female silhouette, so my hands remained calmly still as I sketched the anatomy of the nude model that posed for our art exam.

"Look at the way the natural lighting from the window accentuates her form," our professor instructed.

The seductive model and I stared into each other's eyes as I continued sketching lines of lust. With age I progressed beyond juvenile aerosol cans and phat tip markers to painters' palettes and stretched canvas. As I etched lines of form, the fact that I was a two-time NCAA scoring champ, a three-time High School All-American and the projected number one draft pick in this year's draft meant nothing. Basketball always came easy, like Tracy, Summer, Sofia, Natasha, and all the other girls who had crossed my path.

It could have been my tattoos that offended the alumni, my no-nonsense style of play that rubbed the NCAA wrong or the insane sneaker endorsements I received that caused the media to constantly attempt to ruin my credibility.

"Excellent use of shading Caesar," our Professor commented, startling me from my imagery just in time to scribble the seven numbers the model gestured with her lips.

Who Am I?
I am Baby Jordan...
I am Caesar Gibson.

"Some people get an education without going to college; the rest get it after they get out." – Mark Twain

Acceptance Letter
The Crusaders (Lincoln A. Harris University)

Marquel

"College is like a fountain of knowledge – and the students are there to drink." - Unknown

BEEP… BEEP…BEEP…

I rolled over and slapped my cheap five-dollar alarm clock, fighting the burning sensation coming from my eyes. I still had a few hours before our son Darius woke up, so my wife still lay asleep next to me. I quietly sat up and slipped out from under the covers, making my way to the bathroom.

My skin, the color of a Ghirardelli chocolate square, glistened under the bathroom light. I struggled to get my six-foot frame inside the shower and get ready for another day of lies, deceit and making ends meet.

***

Lincoln A. Harris University (LAHU) was one of the most prestigious Historically Black Colleges in the Southeast. Our attendance was well above FAMU, Bethune Cookman or Morris Brown, our southernmost dominant HBCUs. LAHU sat in the center of Atlanta's "scholarly six": Georgia Tech, Georgia State, Clark, Morehouse, Spellman, and Morris Brown. The new Black Hollywood is what the world considered the city of Atlanta. Young, talented minorities flocked to the city as the thirst for higher education became a priority. We watched as our educational institution grew twenty percent in enrollment over three years, an institution built brick-by-brick by the hands of freed black scholars. With architecture and construction as old and aged as the professors and alumni that still roamed the campus, Lincoln Harris was an institution of higher learning and even higher expectations for its student body.

Campus was buzzing, as it usually did during midday. I took a deep breath of the crisp Atlanta air - an aroma mixture of ripe peaches and orange Georgia clay. Before I could look up I felt two soft hands wrap around my face and cover my eyes.

> "Guess who?"The dreaded question all brothers hated to hear in this situation, knowing the wrong name could get your tires slashed.
> "I'm really not in a guessing mood."
> "Come on! Just guess, silly," the soft voice whispered in my ear.

"Hopefully not the IRS!"

I turned to see Abigail, better known as Ms. June in the new *Atlanta Dymes* calendar. The music video vixen was not only blessed by her mother's design but was also my Body Language regular and steady hook-up at the school bookstore. Knowing Abigail was like having an open bar tab - a privilege you abused until the bartender cut you off.

"Marquel, you know I could do things to you your wife won't?"

Little did Abigail know I had remained faithful to my high school sweetheart, despite what everyone else thought, so I brushed off her comment like normal.

"Where you headed?" she asked.

"You know I got my show at noon."

"Oh yea. That's right," she said in disgust. "You're still playing with that radio stuff, Marquel? Why do you waste your time helping other people with their problems? You need to be working on helping us."

I tried to hide my irritation behind a fake smile and change of topic.

"Whatever, Abigail, you know I love what I do."

"Where's my massage?"

"You know where to find me if you need me," I responded.

"Desire got you and your boys flirting for your money up at Body Language."

Her comment hit me in the stomach like Roy Jones Jr. in his prime.

"Listen, I'm an exotic masseuse and it keeps the bills paid."

"Well, I'm not paying to spend time with you," she said, squeezing my hand.

I pulled away knowing she had a point. If I wanted things to run smoothly I needed to keep her around. Abigail was someone you wanted with you, rather than against you, because you were afraid of the consequences. That was the last thing I heard as I put my hands to my ear giving her the phone gesture.

"Yo kid, Abigail got a phatty!" Queens declared.

"Yea mon, her bamsy big... big... big!" Harlem whispered, causing all of us to laugh at his accent.

"Listen Marquel, why don't you just break her off and avoid the pain and suffering later?" Caesar chimed in slapping everyone dap.

"That's just it - her pain ain't worth suffering over," I reminded.

"Why would he need to cheat when he has that fine wife at home?" Quintin reminded them. "Man, you're just hung up on all those women you get to rub down every day at work," Quintin joked, causing everyone to laugh again.

This was us... This was our Summer Session.

My in-laws were the proudest Puerto Ricans you will ever meet. The problem was my parents were the proudest African Americans on the planet. Two-time Obama voters and secure middle-class, their dream was to have their first-born become a second-generation college grad. I sat through Quinceañera's for my wife's nieces and cousins, was the only black face at Mi Abuela's 70th birthday fiesta, and endured a Marc Anthony concert more than once. Eva was right by my side at Darius' christening, Grandma Lucy's backyard Bar-B-Q and learned to Cha Cha Slide with a Latin flare. This melting pot of cultures inspired me to start BASIK radio, an amateur radio station that became an outlet for me to understand that we are all different and unique for a reason. My outlet transformed into a dominant radio talk show in the Southeast. A show that gave students an opportunity to call in and express themselves about issues around campus, life problems or just to be heard. I became the Michael Baisden of my generation.

I arrived at the station with just enough time to run over the day's show with Chaz. Chaz reminded me of that crazy white boy who was Martin's station engineer at WZUP Radio. He was a colorless soul brother who treated college like a full-time career. He went from GED to MBA in ten party-filled years and was gearing up for another six on a course to get his P.H.D. Chaz and I put the last few details together just seconds before the red on-air light flicked on.

ILLUSTRATIONS

CAESAR

"Tattoos decorate the body but they also decorate the soul." - Unknown

It had nothing to do with women. It was more about maintaining the expectations of the media. I was born with a gift. My large frame, chiseled exterior and charm became a curse at times, so art became my outlet, my escape. Street artists like *Stash*, *Futura*, *DIAM* and *INSA* were legends. Back then we were just junkies for a cinderblock wall to use as a canvas. Finesse and I turned LA into our personal museum. Then one night we decided to get tattoos. We both had original pieces, and I wanted to put mine on my shoulder. That was the night the ink hit my soul.

Marquel, Harlem and Quintin were my family, but my squad was my fraternity. We were a line of five. Our two-guard, Smalls, could pull up from anywhere and bury anything free-throw line extended. Our small forward, Runway, was just that – an attention junkie. He loved the flash of the paparazzi lights and the attention of the microphone during post-game. He was quick on his feet and could knock down the jump shot on the high pick-and-roll. My boy Finesse was the power, my childhood friend and the perfect balance of defense and hustle; he could knock down an open jumper, and he led the NCAA in steals. Anchoring the center was *Big Butta*. His house was that twelve-inch cage below the basket, and his biggest problem was keeping the weight off. He could never follow the team diet restrictions and coach couldn't find a way to slow down the eating. Size was good down low but his weight came along with health problems, something we all worried about. And finally, me... they called me Firm because of how I handled the game and the women off court. Sure, seven other players rounded off Coach Newton's roster but it was the unity of our starting five that made us unstoppable. The hype for this year's season opener was at an all-time high and we handled it the best way we knew how - in the chair of *Art Forms*, Atlanta's hottest tattoo shop. The pool table and full liquor bar broke the stereotypical vibe of traditional tattoo shops. I was running out of real-estate on my frappuccino complexion skin, but unifying team tattoos to start the season were tradition. Alibi, my wizard with a tattoo gun, was on part-two of a four-part original piece I'd drawn and this visit was strictly for shading and touching up.

"You boys got a tough season ahead of you?" Alibi questioned over the hum of the gun.

"Every year they make it harder and every year we keep knocking them down," Runway bragged in his usual manner.

"Two championships in three years is a huge feat but we going hard for number three," I responded, watching the bootleg movie on the flat-screen mounted on the wall.

"Pre-season number one," Smalls reminded the shop, causing everyone to confirm his statement.

"You know they got us playing UCLA in the opener, since they didn't pick you as their top college recruit," Finesse reminded me.

"None of that matters. That was years ago, and staying in Cali was a dead end situation anyway."

"You know the media is going to hype this game up to the 10th power," Butta chimed in with his speech just as slow as it took him to run the court.

"They tried that last year, putting us up against North Carolina, and what happened?"

"Blow out!" All five of us echoed, causing a round of laughter from the shop.

The start of a new school year only meant a new start for the media to put us on a pedestal we worked hard to descend from.

***

There was nothing easy about being the prominent face of LAHU. I stood near the student union doing my best to blend in. The four-carat earring in my ear didn't help, and neither did the tribal tattoo wrapped around my left arm. When I was younger, they made fun of me because I was a lefty. That was before three state championships, three scoring titles and reigning conference leader in assists and rebounds.

"Caesar Gibson?" Two voices asked shyly.

"That's me ladies, and who may you be?"

"I'm Maria."

"And I'm Julia," the two peppy sorority sisters giggled.

"We're really big fans of yours," Julia stated while grabbing my arm like we were walking down the aisle.

"Are you going to take us to the Championship again this year, Caesar?" Maria asked, grabbing the other arm.

"I'm going to try, ladies, but it's good to know I have such... Firm student body support," I responded, looking over their potential and squeezing them closer to my nearly-seven-foot frame.

"We'll be more than rooting, we promise."
They both turned and smiled while walking
away.
I realized at an early age that women became my
much needed escape, an escape from the flashing
cameras, never-ending interviews and mindless
video cameras. My mother, who played the role
of both parents when my ol' man left, raised me. I
grew up around hairdresser gossip and successful,
independent women who weren't afraid to voice
their unhappiness for deadbeat men. It was only
natural I grew up knowing all the right words,
applied the right charm and developed the right
touch. I was introduced to nieces,
granddaughters, and sometimes their own flesh
and blood due to my allure.
The story always begins with that first love, or
that first crush. Mine was Kasmeria Davis, the
daughter of my mother's best friend. She was
half-black, half-Latina, so her skin was the color
of Christmas eggnog. Only two years separated us
in age, but my charm and height made it easy for
her to mistake me for an average 16-year-old.
Before her, basketball was all I knew. Summer
camps, daily practice and AAU junior leagues
became routine, so it was refreshing to discover
infatuation for something other than a Spalding
ball. I lost my virginity and endured my first
heartbreak all in the same summer. When I look
back at it, she was that small pebble in the snow
that created this out of control snowball.

Soundtrack Of My Life

Quintin

"Men do the things they do to become the men they need to become." - Unknown

My little brother Quincy was the future. He was the defiant me. Wanted to be everything I wasn't: bad. Wrong crowd, wrong choices and my parent's worst nightmare. He decided to follow in my father's footsteps and enlist in the Army straight out of high school. He was my right hand, so I worried about him every time we heard another US soldier was killed on the news. Last I heard, his unit was deployed again with the second surge. I wrote him once a month, since this tour was going to be much longer than the first.

I stood impatiently in the campus work-study line, waiting to complete my paperwork for the semester. The new pair of *SB Dunks* on my feet matched perfectly with the *UNDEFEATED* shirt that was partially tucked between my jeans and belt buckle. My wireless *Beatz by Dre* headphones were tucked into the back pocket of my jeans that hung slightly off my waist. Lengthy lines stretched with students needing government aid to pay for an overpriced education, but today's visit was only to find an on-campus job to help offset the cost of my final semester. The *iPod* in my pocket was blaring the new NAS album and my patience was wearing thin with our administrative staff.

I wasn't used to the slower pace of the South. I was still used to wearing my *Timberlands* untied, a crisp white tee and sweats in the summer. The thought of a mouth full of gold and mispronounced words just wasn't my style. Down south everyone replaced "street slang" with a "country twang," and if you didn't listen closely you could miss an entire phrase or comment. Only time can create change, and in three short years, I found my niche in the dirty South, and life closer to the equator began to grow on me.

***

My major was Education, but the way they treated teachers made the last three years at Lincoln Harris a complete waste of time. It was true we never did it for the money, but the real return was in the faces of the kids, whose lives I affected every day. My goal after graduation was to become a high school music teacher. But without my degree I was stuck in the substitute teacher system, roaming from school to school teaching whatever grade level needed a fill-in. I was super excited when our campus work-study program needed a preschool music teacher. LAHU empowered parenting students by providing separate on-campus housing and childcare to ease their path to graduation. I was even more excited when Marquel and Eva told me my Godson Darius was going to be in my class.

Today was comprised of meeting the preschool director, getting the key for my classroom, and hopefully having a little time to set things up before my first group of kids arrived.

"Mr. Bennet? Pleasure to meet you," Dr. Newman, the preschool director, asked with her rich Southern accent.

"Dr. Newman?" I reassured her by extending my hands in a warm welcome.

"Mr. Bennet, our preschool has a dress code for our teachers," she responded.

Her accent was thick and rich like it was mixed with molasses and sweet tea. The grey in her hair stood out like years of wisdom, and her comment sounded like my Grandmother's philosophy.

"Since this is your first day, I will let it slide, but here are the teacher/student guidelines and curriculum for the school year."

I was a little shocked by her abrasiveness and fumbled for a response; I took the paperwork and a seat. Today, I traded in my usual *Nike* footwear for some boat loafers, found the least baggy pair of jeans in my closet and ironed the one button-down shirt that my mom gave me years ago.

"You will have three scheduled classes to teach a day and we have been in contact with the dean of your college to ensure that your classes are scheduled around your employment here."

The seriousness of her tone made this simple on-campus opportunity until graduation feel like a real job.

"Here are the keys to your classroom and the keys to the music cabinet that holds all of our instruments."

I took the keys with a smile, excited to have access to musical instruments.

"Our staff will be expecting you in the lounge for introductions in 30 minutes so I would settle in your classroom and join us at that time."

I was still taking all of her information in, shaking my head and thinking a million questions but couldn't muster a word.

"Oh, and Mr. Bennet, what are you doing with your hair?"

Her question was again filled with a mixture of confusion and sarcasm that I patted my cornrows, mumbling,

"My hair is a mess, I know, I'll have it re-braided this weekend."

The inside of my classroom was just enough. The walls were thin but that was only a problem for the other teachers. Windows in the corner let in some natural lighting, giving the room a warm feeling, but the naked walls screamed for posters of Miles Davis, Marvin Gaye and Bob Marley. I sat on the corner of my desk taking it all in until the sound of the door opening broke my enjoyment.

"Hey, sorry to interrupt, just thought I'd walk you over to the lounge, maybe give you a lay of the land before you walk into that room filled with estrogen."

"I'm Quintin...Quintin Bennet," I stood to greet.

"Damn, you wore jeans on your first day? I bet Dr. Newman was pissed," he responded, shocked at my appearance.

"I'm Mr. Little, Dante Little the PE teacher, and you my friend have the biggest balls I have ever seen."

His statement made us both break out in laughter.

"Her ship is that tight, huh?" I acknowledge, confirming that my first impression was my worst.

"She's a tough nut, but has a soft spirit. You just have to get on her good side."

"Well, what else should I know before I walk in there?"

"Ms. Ross and Ms. DeVaughn are our resident cougars; they've been here the longest and prey on the only two men on the staff – me and now you, my friend."

"Really?"

"Let's just say they're the reason we need a new music teacher."

"Wow."

"Mrs. Castle is married but extremely cute. She's a harmless kitten and our new art teacher starts today, so I'll be meeting her for the first time today – Ms. Jones, I believe. My only hope is she's young and single."

We were in front of the lounge as he wrapped up his overview.

"You even got a head full of cornrows," he chuckled, shaking his head in disbelief.

I wanted to crawl in a hole once I realized I broke half of the director's rules on my first day.

The sounds of welcome snapped me back to reality as Mr. Little opened the door to the teachers' lounge.

The Empire

Harlem

"Opportunity dances with those already on the dance floor." – H. Jackson Brown, Jr.

We made it acceptable by calling it a "Jamaican themed" flash mob. A part of me felt bad for having to water down the culture for profit but at a certain age it became about survival. The real trick to our success was our ability to be all inclusive, cross social class, adaptable, White, Black, Asian, Hispanic. We listened to everyone's music, read everyone's paper and watched everyone's sport so we knew how to communicate; how to fit in. We were the 21st century distributors. No more shady backdoor, sloppy scale, sandwich bag operations. We were "The Empire" and we had exactly four months to get our routine ready for *Tropics,* the biggest Dancehall competition this side of the equator. This year's competition would be hosted by our very own Lincoln A. Harris University Caribbean

Student Organization, so the stakes were extremely high. Every major HSBU would send their finest teams to compete for the title which my crew held with much esteem. But today's meeting wasn't about the competition it was about business.

I watched as everyone filled the tiny room. The abandoned warehouse was filled with cobwebs and walls thick enough to restrain secrets. We only met like this once a month, but it was something that had to be done to keep business running smoothly. The East side of town was maintained by *Cardinal* and *Squeeze*, two of my most loyal and oldest soldiers. They were my *Express* boys, Modern fit 42 regular type dudes that ran business as smoothly as they dressed. They were uptown guys I put in charge of membership and background checks for the business; they also took care of our posh Gorgonian clientele. *20/20* and *Allure,* our only female, ran the Westside of town with responsibilities on police Intel and location scouting. During the day we were known for our rhythmic synchronized dancing skill, but by night we became an unstoppable force providing a supply for a growing demand. The four of us handled business for years until the expansion and popularity of the urban Atlanta area. The controlled concentration of six colleges and universities combined with the overwhelming amount of clubs, college kids and young entrepreneurs changed the magnitude of our operation over time. We began to take on soldiers who could handle money and keep their mouths shut. *Messiah* took care of the athletes, *Shaa'* managed the fraternities and sororities while *Felony* took care of any regular nine-to-five local and faithful customers around the area. All three polar opposites: Messiah was the oldest and with his age came wisdom and logic. Shaa' was my gateway to the Southern clientele; I learned early that business was run differently North to South just as it was East to West. In the South it was the "Trap" and you had to be accepted to run business there. Shaa' was my in. *Felony...* Felony, was the loose cannon, the X-factor, "the problem."

The eight of us gathered in a small abandoned building on the Eastside of town. We rotated locations every month to keep law enforcement on their toes.

"Welcome everyone," I announced as Felony and Shaa' finally got to their seats.
I sat in my seat putting the finishing touches on my re-rolled Dutch Master while scanning the room at what I'd created. My empire rested in the hands of these seven individuals. Since I never dealt directly with hand-to-hand transactions, these were the folks taking all the risk. I let each of them run there section of town however they

felt fit; as long as they kept the attention off us and kept Dr. Bird and Legacy's money coming in on time.

"Harlem, there's crazy money flowing through this city," Squeeze shouted with excitement.

Everyone agreed and sat silently as the room filled with a thick smoke.

"We grossed $200,000 this week, real champion money." I announced to the group.

"That's a lot of cash," Allure said realizing that we were bringing in twice as much money as we did just a year ago.

I agreed and took a long drag of my blunt.

"I brought you all here for a different reason." I announced causing them all to pay closer attention.

"In a month's time we will have enough of our own product to sever our dependence on Dr. Bird and Legacy."

The weight of my statement settled in with the silence that followed.

"Bout time!" Felony announced followed by agreement from Shaa' and 20/20.

"You think that's a good idea Harlem?" Messiah questioned already using his wisdom to foresee what I was expecting.

"He's not going to be too happy to see his money coming up short," Allure chimed in more worried about the consequences I'd face than all of them.

"I've thought about this long and hard, our grow houses will be mature and ready for distribution this time next month and you all are looking at increases in your profits in the thousands."

That statement changed the energy in the room for the better.

"Here we go," Cardinal and Squeeze perked up exchanging dap at the sound of cash.

"With more money comes more sufferation," I announced. "We are constantly working to stay one step ahead of Babylon so be aware that we will be adding Dr. Bird and Legacy to the list of our enemy's, it's only a matter of time before they start getting close. I called you all here today because I want to advise you all to start stashing for hard times."

"Stashing for what?" Felony asked foreseeing where this was heading.

"This business, all we've worked for. We should all start looking to protect our investments now."

I realized what I was asking these guys to give up, a $5,000 a week gig that required little to no experience.

"I see where you're coming from Harlem," 20/20 spoke up. "But we all have too much invested in this to just stop."

"Yea, that new Mercedes is coming out real soon, and I'm only a few grand away from buying it cash," Messiah said, followed by a round of laughter.

"We're all getting money, and there is plenty more in our future" I said exhaling another thick puff of smoke. "We all must keep our eyes open or things can easily get washed away."

"We do have a minor problem I would like to bring to everyone's attention," Shaa' announced. "We have a new local distributor that refuses to partner with the Empire."

Past experience with local dealers caused me to listen more attentively.

"His name?" I inquired slightly concerned.

"They call him Faze and he's a youngster that shoots first asks questions last."

I sat back in my chair as all eyes fell on me in my moment of reflection.

"This meeting is adjourned," I announced as everyone slowly got up and left, confused at my lack of reaction.

Little did they know my mind had already shifted into damage control mode.

DOUBLE ZERO

QUINTIN

"As if you could kill time without injuring eternity." - Henry David Thoroeau

I was only eight when Spelling and her folks stopped by for game night. My folks set up a weekly competition for the residence on the block as a get to know each other opportunity. Come to find out they were hustling the entire neighborhood out of their paychecks on payday.

> "You play dominos?" I asked too shy to look her in the face.
> "A little bit," she said taking the pack from me with a smile.

That was the night that we played and laughed; we laughed and fell in love. We were too young to know it then, but our friendship grew stronger every day after that game. It helped that our mothers took a liking to each other so we looked forward to our weekly visits. Then one day she took my lucky double-blank piece and wrote her phone number on the back.

***

There was something juvenile about calling it a club. It was wingtip sophistication, expensive torpedo cigars, weekender bags filled with cash. The day was almost over by the time I pulled open the door to *Intentions*, a decent-size lounge across the street from campus. My ace, Dee opened the spot a few years ago, not knowing the music played within those walls would eventually be the perfect marriage between Jazz and Soul music; the Harlem Renaissance fused with Don Cornelius aboard the Soul Train, Chaka Khan meets Beyonce' meets Erykah Badu type spot. Dee always had real up-and coming artists do guest appearances and that element gave the place character, a New York Undercover vibe. The real essence however happened on the tables above the stage, above the mellow vibe and easy listeners. The small section was the gambling lounge with huge buy-in's and only for Atlanta's young up-and-coming. Some liked Roulette, some loved Craps and many liked Poker but my game was Dominos. The sound of Alicia Keys latest hit reverberated through the large speakers mounted in the corners of the lounge. The few people gathered inside were all bobbing their heads in unison to the rhythmic new beat.

"Sup Queens," Dee yelled as he spotted me walking in.

I smiled, because Dee never used my government name, only nicknames he concocted at the spur of the moment.

"What's the science, Dee?"

"Same shit, different day, playboy"

"I can dig it," I said walking over and giving him dap.

Intentions became an escape from the real world; I would come in here between classes and just tune myself out playing young up & comers. I won more than I lost, that was the trick. *Always quit when your ahead.* Dominos were a way of life; I grew up watching three generations of my family hustle the numbers for money.

"You were on fire the other night Q; had this entire place holding their breath with that last competition! Everybody was praying you pulled it out."

"Say Word!" I said with a slight grin.

"Marquel told me you were teaching the kids music over at the preschool."

I was caught off guard by his ability to go from compliment to admiration so easily.

"Yea, it's going to be a great opportunity for me to enhance my resume before I graduate."

"I just wanted to let you know I think that's a great thing you're doing?"

The seriousness of his statement made me stop and take notice.

"Thanks man," I acknowledged, giving my pursuit to teach better meaning.

My grandfather once told me the secret to happiness is to *find something you're good at and find a way to make money doing it*; so dominos became the second side to my playing piece of life. I later found out that my grandparents were also known as the Bonny and Clyde of dominos back in the 60's. They would have dreams of my father following in their footsteps and made him next in line for the throne. He was good, but despite their intentions he became the first college graduate of the family. With that degree he moved us out of New York to suburban Atlanta. A big house with a big lawn and Southern hospitality to raise his family - the only problem was the domino skills flowed through my veins.

***

It was Thursday night...

Why Thursday night?

That was the only day Caesar had early practice, the only day Harlem didn't have rehearsal, and the only day any of us could carve out time to catch up with each other. Marquel was kind enough to let us crash his place since we were all still on campus. This was how we kept in touch; over 28 dominos is how we communicated - this was Thursday night.

"Harlem, you made it,"

"Ya dun know, I can't miss Thursday nights... tradition," he uttered in his thickest accent.

We both arrived at Marquel's place at the same time.

"Fellas... Fellas... Fellas," Marquel announced opening the door with beers in hand. The playful sounds of his son Darius echoed in the background.

"Wsup Uncle Harlem, Uncle Quintin?"
He asked in his grown up toddler body.
"When you guys going to let me play?"
"Boy! If you don't get your fast behind out
of here?" Marquel shooed him off.
"Wsup gentlemen?"
"Living the life," I responded causing us to
chuckle at his sarcasm.
"Caesar coming?"
"He should be here shortly; you know it's
Tanya Thursday," Marquel reminded.
We all broke out again in laugher. The sound of
his doorbell ringing startled us.
"I heard that," Caesar announced ducking
to get into the doorway not amused by the
accuracy of the statement.
"Damn, these dorm room doors are paper
thin," Marquel reminded us.
We all laughed again at the accuracy of the
statement.
"Can't teach an old dog new tricks,"
Marquel reminded us.
"Wsup Uncle Cease"
"Wsup lil' man?"
"Darius, isn't it time for bed?" Marquel
commanded signaling it was time to get
started.
We took our seats as I washed the deck.
"How's married life," Caesar asked, taking
a jab at Marquel who was in a debate with
his wife in the other room.
"Go ahead and eat without me!" he
shouted. "It's Thursday, we playing!"

"Blood Clot," Harlem hissed obviously flustered by his hand early.

"So what's going on with everyone?"

"Darius turns four in a few weeks and his mother has a huge party planned, you all better be there." Marquel reminded us slapping his piece down.

As if him or his wife Eva would let either of us forget.

"Just remind wifey not to put it on the same weekend as *Tropics*," Harlem reminded. Slapping his piece down with more effort.

"I'm there."

"They said their coming baby!" He yelled off in the distance.

"Why would you place that piece Q," Caesar questioned since tonight we were playing in teams and my early move had my partner puzzled.

"Have no fear oh tall and popular one," I bowed to him in my horrible Mr. Miyagi impression.

"How are things going with business Harlem?" Caesar asked.

"All fruits ripe man," he mumbled, pissed.

We all laughed when he got like that.

"What did he just say?" Caesar asked knowing exactly why we were laughing.

"Unu blood seed!" Harlem yelled excited. Obviously walking into the trap my earlier move created.

"Hey Marquel, when you going to tell that sexy wife of yours what you do at Body Language?" Caesar asked, finally getting his revenge for his earlier comment.

"When you can tell us who your real father is..."

"Jesus!" Harlem responded in his deepest accent to the comment.

"I'ight guys, let's take it easy," I jumped in sensing they were both throwing low blows.

The two of them were always at odds probably because Marq was better at withstanding temptation than Caesar was. We all knew the quantity and quality of women that Marquel had access to through Body Language and the fact that he was able to remain faithful to his wife was a sign of strength - while some saw it as a sign of weakness.

"You guys ready for the season?" Harlem asked trying to bring things back.

"Yea mon!" Caesar tried with his phony Jamaican accent.

"You better, the point spread on your season opener is unreal and I need a "W" from you boys to win big!"

"You know you can't tell me stuff like that Harlem."

"Whatever, I'm just keeping it real... no pressure."

"When's the next big tournament?" Marquel asked.

"Dee is lining something big so ya'll stay tuned."

"Good, the busier you guys are the more revenue I can bring in," Harlem reminded us.

My final statement was followed by the finale of my move to seal the game for Caesar and I.

"How the hell did you do that?" Marquel asked puzzled.

"See that's why it's unfair to play with unu blood clot!" Harlem mumbled having to shuffle the pieces.

B.A.S.I.K
(Brothers and Sisters Immerse In Knowledge)

MARQUEL

If life is a journey then I never want to stop exploring.

The inside of a college textbook can quickly become a strange place. Never mind the $60 price tag, endless chapters of unreadable ten-point font or the additional required supplemental guide; the best lessons I came to realize were sometimes life learned.

Message

My iPhone alerted me. I glanced at the screen and noticed the text messages from Denise and a Facebook alert from Carmen, two of my favorite clients from Body Language.

.

> **Carmen:** I enjoyed our get-together yesterday
> **Young Denzel:** I'm glad I could satisfy my clients
> **Carmen:** Is that all I am, your client?

I held off on my response because Carmen's obsession helped buy my books this semester and pushed my twitter following up an extra thousand. I didn't want my response to rock the boat already on calm seas.

Denise: When can you schedule me in for another appointment, I've been dying to see you again.
Young Denzel: I have some time on Friday if you can wait until then.

I smiled because Denise single-handedly contributed to Darius' new wardrobe, pampers and Pre-K tuition. There was no telling what else I could sway by spending some time with her right before the weekend. There was no right or wrong, this was college... this was survival.

I ended my conversation by quietly taking a seat in the back of my Black Studies class.
"Now class, the black studies movement began when significant numbers of black students enrolled in predominantly white institutions for the first time," Professor Royce explained.
I considered this semester my semester of upliftment. I purposely filled my curriculum with as many black studies courses I could find in our course guide. I enrolled in *Journey into African American Music 4020*, second hour with Quintin. Then off to *Exploration of the Black Diaspora*

4029, third and fourth hour, followed by *The Cost of Freedom 3545* and *Journey into Hip Hop 3030*. After that it was off to the station to host B.A.S.I.K. in the afternoon. Professor Royce was one of my favorite professors because of his passion for the progression of our people. I listened as he continued with today's lecture.

"Black students understood that education was essential to empowerment. In 1967 black students accounted for only two percent of the total enrollment at predominantly white colleges and universities."

I just sat and soaked up all the knowledge that resided in our history. Most of the information I absorbed in my classes was used as ammunition for my radio show.

* * *

"This is B.A.S.I.K. radio and today's topic is the cost of freedom," I yelled into the microphone.

"Caller you're on the air, let us know what your freedom cost?"

"This is Veronica, and to all those cheap negro's out there, they need to know that my freedom cost at least a dinner and a movie."

Her comment caused me and Chaz to break out in laughter.

"Thank you Veronica, let's not forget how much a dinner and a movie cost nowadays,

I hope you're at least letting him get to second base with those kind of requirements."

"Next caller you're on the air, tell us what your freedom costs?"

"This is Neal and I think the correct answer to your question is freedom cost the struggle of the Freedom Rights movement, lynching, beatings, sit-in and years of oppression."

"That's a great response Neal," I responded. "But there is no right or wrong answer to this question, Freedom means a lot of things to many people. To some, it means that women will no longer be sexually exploited. Freedom could mean having the opportunity to read and write or not having to obtain permission to move around the country."

Chaz gave me a look of approval with my response and I was inspired to close the show off on a high note.

"Here we stand on the edge of the twenty-first century and still we are not free, what does freedom cost my brothers and sisters? Immerse yourself in knowledge, I'm your host Marquel Howard and this is B.A.S.I.K radio."

Chaz did his normal thing on the console and cued in some commercials to conclude our show for the afternoon.

ART IMITATES LIFE

CAESAR

"Of all the worldly passions, lust is the most intense"
- Buddha

The library during mid-day was a hotbed for intelligent women seeking solitude within the confines of dusty books and outdated computers. Sophia and I sat across from each other with our heads buried in our Art history books. I sat scribbling a silhouette of my personal teaching assistant who could teach a bum to be a billionaire. Sophia was from Trinidad, so her complexion was rich like Bailey's Irish Cream. Her physique was thick as if she had played field hockey for years and when she talked, the sexiest accent would dance from her lips. Sophia was what I called Mount Everest; an unconquerable mountain. No amount of game or charm could loosen the chastity belt that hung from her powerful hips. Our relationship was strictly schoolwork and grades, but how I wanted a taste of her sugarcane.

"What are you looking at Caesar?" she asked, catching me taking her all in.

"I'm just admiring the possibilities."

"Whatever Caesar, you're so full of it, let me see what you're drawing, cause your obviously not doing any work" she asked stealing my rough sketch.

"Wow, this is good. Are you sure basketball is your calling?"

"Right now your body's….calling…," I sang in my worst R Kelly impersonation.

"Caesar, please. What happened to Dion? Weren't you two dating?"

"Dion! Please, she wasn't my type, plus our team nicknamed her "Kit Kat"."

"Kit Kat? Why Kit Kat?"

"Cause she would "break anybody off a piece of that…"

Sophia, broke out in laughter at the analogy.

"Then what about that cute volleyball player Ava?"

"Who, jealous Ava? I heard before she broke up with her ex she took his chap stick, rubbed it between her legs then gave it back to him so he could kiss his new girl with those lips."

"Scandalous!" she said in disgust.

"Look we could go on and on with this Q&A session, but the bigger picture here is me and you."

"The bigger picture here is this homework, so let's get focused Caesar."

And just like that we were back to square one; victory Sophia.

Looking back at my extensive female catalog, there was marching band Isabella, who caused traffic pileup's any time she crossed the street, but she was addicted to nicotine and narcotics so her bad habits eventually outweighed her drop-dead looks. My Saintly church girl Destiny, who brought new meaning to the word "God Body," helped me get in touch with a spiritual side I never knew I had. That's until the lights went out, then we committed every cardinal sin in the Bible. That ended abruptly when I found out she was the Pastors daughter. Then there was Madison, the shy librarian. For months I couldn't find anything wrong with her and was intrigued by her intelligence and shyness. Then one day I received a threatening call from one of her baby's father's. Then I found out Madison was a fertile machine that got pregnant at the site of sperm. Four kids and three baby fathers later I found myself in the middle of her love Triangle drowning.

"Caesar... Caesar!"

I came back to reality with the sound of Sophia whispering my name.

"Now that's a sound I can get used to." I responded, causing her to blush.

Buzz... Buzz

The vibration of my S4 ruined another opportunity to flatter her with my game.

> **SnkrConnect:** I got the new Retro VI in stock, you coming bye to pick up your pair?

This had to be Crystal, the manager at our local sneaker spot. Crystal was a 30-year-old district manager with a yearning to remain young. There would be lines of young teenagers camping out in front of her store to buy sneakers days in advance, but I was awarded the luxury of walking-in and out with no wait.
"Who's that, another girl?"
"Naw, my sneaker connect giving me the inside scoop."
"You got like a hundred pair of sneakers, why do you need more? You don't even wear half of them anyway."

Truthfully it was more like eight hundred pairs. There was something in the paint. I'd inhale the scent of a deadstock pair and exhale the ecstasy of having. Sometimes just owning a certain pair of sneakers could earn the right of passage into a covert underground society of collectors that evolved from daily chat board researchers to early morning campout seekers. Something as simple as a sneaker had evolved way beyond just a gym shoe. In some cases it was a symbol of who you were, or how much you would spend to become that someone. The footwear industry consumed those that fed off of fashion, popularity and prestige. *Envy rested on the minds of those who chose to walk with their heads down seeking what they could not obtain.*

> "Sophia, how about we pick this up tomorrow? I got a lot on my mind and I'm just not focused on work right now."
> "That's cool, I'm getting tired too."

We both packed up our things and promised to call each other later to re-schedule our study session.

Just as I was crossing the street to get back to my dorm, an egg-shell white X5 pulled up. I stood there mesmerized by the twenty-four inch rims. The limo tinted window slid down and a dark skinned brother wearing a suit shouted,

> "Mr. Patten wants to see you."
> *The Sports Agent?* I thought.

I opened the door and slid in the giant SUV with ease, the driver looked young but very mature. The suit he wore was well tailored and his dress shoes were shining like he had just got them polished from that booth in a train station.

"Nice car you got here," I stated trying to spark a little conversation.

The driver never took his eyes off the road and didn't say a word to me the entire ride. We pulled up in front of a high rise building downtown that reflected the sun from its glass walls.

"Follow me," the brother finally broke his silence putting the truck in park.

We walked through the revolving glass doors and headed straight to the elevators. He pushed the top floor and we stood in silence again as the elevator doors shut to begin its ascent.

The chime of the elevator and the catchy music playing amused me until the doors opened to a huge office filled with light. This office was more like a penthouse; it had a lounge, a kitchen area, and a small living room with a flat screen in the center. Autographed sneakers, posters, plaques and trophies where scattered throughout the house.

"Mr. Gibson, how nice of us to finally meet," he said extending his hand.

"My name is Charles Patten."

For an average sized guy, his handshake was strong. Mr. Patten wore what seemed to be a very expensive suit and came across as a person who lived life from a Blackberry.

"Please follow me," he said headed toward the back of the penthouse.

He swung open two doors that lead to another room filled with high-tech equipment. He pointed to a large swivel chair that sat in front of a presidential looking desk.

"Please, have a seat," he instructed.

Behind his desk were TV's, computer monitors, and even a sports ticker. He looked like he had a mini Wall Street going on right in his Penthouse.

"I'm going to cut right to the chase, Caesar, I am a Sports Agent. Correction, I am the best Sports Agent there is in the business. I've been watching you ever since you went from ordinary to extraordinary and today I am going to make you an offer you may want to give some serious consideration."

I was used to this pitch and waited to hear his offer.

"I need you to help me give the Crusaders their first loss during the season opener in a few weeks."

His request caught me off guard and I was confused and shocked all at the same time.

"First, let's start by saying that you have led the Crusaders to two straight undefeated seasons, an outstanding accomplishment. But the spread on the season opener has Lincoln Harris by +15 and a loss would mean a lot of money for me and my business partners who have put a substantial amount on your opponents UCLA."

"So you're asking me to lose the game on purpose?" I asked for clarification.

I watched as Mr. Patten sat back in his chair, watching the puzzled look that covered my face.

"I'm sure you have some questions Mr. Gibson. Why don't you take some time and think it over."

"In the mean time, here is my card, you can call me anytime."

I got up and headed towards the front of his penthouse.

"Oh! Mr. Gibson, I was told you had a thing for sneakers and fine art, here is a little something to show my appreciation for taking time out to see me today," pointing at his driver who was now holding a silver brief case.

The B.M. dropped me off exactly where I was picked up. I was left standing on the corner holding the briefcase and staring right at trouble; Mr. Patten's business card.

CHARACTER FLAW

QUINTIN

"Four wheels move the body. Two wheels move the soul." – unknown

Ya Ya Dacosta, Zoe Saldana, Rosario Dawson – It may sound crazy but this is how I remembered the names of three classes filled with twelve rambunctious kids every day. Their look, their personalities, their mannerisms just reminded me of certain "A list" celebrities I'd grown to admire. I made it through my first few weeks of Dr. Newman's rigorous school year. My rough New York look was replaced with a more laid back J.Crew vibe. It was a change I made when Lance Gross in my 2:00 class started dressing in clothes that looked like mine. I didn't realize how silly I looked until a six year old tried to emulate me. Then it hit me - *These kids are watching, listening.* I needed a new more influential look that sent them a positive way to earn respect.

"I like the tie Mr. Bennet," she complimented.

"Thanks Dr. Newman," I smiled.

My smile quickly turned to concern as Ms. Ross and Ms. DeVaughn slithered over with lust in their eyes.

"Mr. Bennet," they both whispered tugging and pulling at my arms.

"Ladies," I responded trying to brush them off.

"Do you have a girlfriend... seeing someone... have any friends with benefits?"

I laughed at their comments and surveyed the hall for my escape. I found Ms. Jones room to my right and maneuvered my way out of their clutch.

"It was a pleasure ladies but I have to ask Ms. Jones something," I explained shutting the door before my sentence could finish.

"What did you need to ask me?"

I turned to face Ms. Jones and cleared my throat.

"Oh! Nothing... I was trying to get away from Ms. Ross and Ms. DeVaughn."

"Oh, those two," she replied already hip to the game.

I laughed and took a moment to take her in – she was stunning.

"Art, huh?" I questioned, looking around her room trying to hide my attraction.

"Music, huh?" she responded, looking me over.

"Nice tie,"
I blushed.

"Thank You." I responded fleeing just as
quickly as I entered.
Class started in two-minutes and I didn't want to
be late.

***

The smell of burnt tires and gasoline fumes filled
the night air of downtown Atlanta. Harlem, Dee,
Chaz and I stood amongst the Up-North riders
burning and talking trash. It was three in the
morning on a Friday, which meant riders from all
over the A.T.L. would line the streets to show off
their bikes and race the streets for supremacy.
The segregation of riders was apparent up and
down Peachtree Boulevard as low-rider bikes sat
separate from stock bikes. Black, White and
Latino riders were huddled in their familiar
groups. Even amongst the Blacks, the up-north
crew distanced themselves from the down-south
riders, female riders distance themselves from
their male counterparts leaving the night air filled
with tension.

"Looks like another hot night, huh fellas?"
I asked passing the spliff back to Harlem.
"Certainly is," Dee agreed, taking a look
up and down the block at just how many
people had gathered for *7 Sins* bike night.
"Hell of a night," Harlem chimed in
keeping an eye on his foot soldiers making
their rounds through the crowd.

The four of us stood in the middle of the biker cipher surrounded by customized bikes that would put Xzibit's show to shame. Broadway, the leader of the crew, sat in the center of his team laughing and taking in the atmosphere.

"Pass that here Harlem," Broadway demanded snatching the blunt.

"Only because you're my people I'm going to let you snatch my trees, if I didn't know you I would've let my goons loose all over you." Harlem responded causing everyone to break out in laughter.

"Whatever Rasta."

"Stop messing with him baby," Majesty requested.

Majesty was Broadway's dime piece who sat exotically on the back of his bike. Majesty was a half Black/half Brazilian bombshell who deserved her own cover on *SHOW Magazine*.

"So when you getting a bike Q?" she asked me seductively.

"You know I prefer the safety of four wheels and leather interior."

"I second that," Chaz chimed in giving me dap in acknowledgement.

"Don't knock it until you try it," Sham spoke up; his Mets fitted tilted slightly over his brow matching the colors of his bike.

"Enough about bikes, what's good with some of your girls Majesty?" I asked growing impatient with the sausage fest quickly developing.

"Damn Q, their on the way, be patient" she insisted leaning over to take the joint from Broadway.

I watched as she put the chocolate blunt, the size of a mini sharpie, to her lips and inhaled slowly. The five of us all stared in amazement wishing we could be the smoke that danced across her soft skin.

"Harlem we've got a problem." Harlem's right-hand man Felony announced making his way through the crowd.

"It's Faze, he's working his way up the block and stepping all over our product and clientele in the process."

"What!"

We all focused our direction down the block to see Faze and his two-man team making their way towards us.

"Let's go see if we can talk some sense into our good friend Faze?" Harlem said shaking his head and making his way in their direction. The four of us followed preparing for the worst.

"Where'd you get this from? Listen I'll sell you this for half that price... The Empire! Please you aint smoked nothing like this before."

We could hear Faze and his two goons trashing Harlem's crew and their product as we approached.

"Faze, what can I do for you?" Harlem asked startling him from his weak sales pitch.

His skin was a southern brown, richened from working the blocks during the summer heat. His mouth was filled with gold and when he spoke you had to listen carefully because of his deep southern drawl. He was a local small-time drug dealer and despised Harlem and his crew for taking all of the local consumers. As we stood there the smell of cheap weed and liquor seeped from his pores. The white tee he wore had turned a strange beige and you could see his socks through the fake translucent sneakers on his feet.

"Well look what we have here fellas!" Faze announced to his two do-boys Lookout and Standby.

"Wsup son?" Standby mocked in his worst New York impression.

"Look here cuz, this right hur is our streets," Faze declared.

"Yea, and you messing up our money," Lookout chimed in.

Lookout and Standby were two funny characters. Both rocked unkept locks that desperately needed re-twisting and oversized knock off clothes that were a bit over the top.

"Listen fellas, we don't want any trouble," Felony spoke up breaking the tension between the awkward standoff.

"Yea so why don't yall keep it moving?" I spoke up getting irritated with their ignorance.

"We got us a big problem here cuz, my money's coming up real short since your crew started moving in on our territory."

"There's plenty of money to be made out here, let's work something out so we all can line our pockets." Harlem responded.

We could all see the tension and frustration building in the amateur duffle bag crew which caused us all to knuckle up. Noticing they were easily outnumbered the three musketeers backed down from the lob sided beat down.

"Another time, another place," Lookout proclaimed as they made their way across the street to continue their hustle.

We all broke out in laughter as we headed back to Broadway and his crew, all of us but Harlem who kept an eye on Faze and his boys.

"You headed back man?" I asked.

"Yea, I'm just a little worried at what's standing across the street."

"What's that, phony ass Faze and his crew?"

"No...trouble."

Broadway and his crew were clowning other bikers by the time we made it back. The thunderous sound of well tuned engines approached us as we imitated Faze and his boys. Majesty, familiar with the sound, perked up with excitement as five slender bikers approached us. They pulled right into the center of Broadway's crew and turned off their engines in unison. Majesty jumped off Broadway's bike to greet her girls. Harlem and I watched attentively at the mysterious riders who suddenly demanded our attention. The leader of the crew removed her lid and slowly un-mounted her bike. I watched in amazement as her skinny jeans hugged her waist and thighs like a musical eight note. The crisp Flint Jordan VII's on her feet matched the white Kid Robot t-shirt that sported a cute bear on the front.

"Nia!" Majesty screamed, barely giving her a chance to straighten herself out.

I watched as they shared a friendly embrace and turned to the rest of her crew. Some were replacing their slips for high heels, while others were straightening out their hair and makeup. Nia's team was stunning; many of them looked as if they had just come from the runways of Paris or a photo shoot for *America's Next Top Model*.

"Damn!" Chaz whispered taking in the same scenery I did.

Majesty corralled her girls once they finished their gossip and giggles and led them over to us.

"Quintin this is…"

"Ms. Jones," I finished her sentence.

I didn't even notice the confusion on her face when Nia responded.

"Mr. Bennet," with a smile.

We stood there for a moment admiring and smiling.

"Nice to meet you," I responded, extending my hand like we were strangers.

"Pleasure to meet you too," she said returning the embrace.

We both could feel the eyes of everyone but heard nothing.

"So this is what you do when you're not teaching art?"

"So this is what you do when you're not playing with musical instruments all day?"

I Did...

MARQUEL

"All men make mistakes, married men just find out about them sooner." - unknown

When I was younger I was selfish. I guess we all are in some form or fashion, but more so in our youth than in adulthood. I learned to keep secrets early but that turned out to be more of a nuisance than a benefit. The funny thing was, Body Language was the perfect place for me to stray, but I realized quickly that a way to a women's heart was not through the physical, but through the emotional. While Denim, Zoe', and the Mayor filled their pockets by pleasing women sexually, I invested in "quality time" for the long term. The real money was in listening, intellectual conversation and an occasional shoulder to lean on. The sure way to build a clientele of loyal return customers was as simple as paying attention, listening to their issues, or simply just caring. So much of that had been washed out like

Tsunami's when the internet became the next big thing.
Just think... it was all just a click away!

EVERYTHING!

You needed to know how to pick a lock... check the internet. You needed to figure out exactly what Southernplayalisticadillacmuzik meant... check the internet. Learn the moves to Gundam Style... check the internet. Body Language was a place to turn emotions into profit. I never cheated on my wife, I was proud to hang my hat on that, yet I was Body Language's most requested, most sought after and most loved. The catch - a winning formula like that can only lead to deep, severe and sometimes extreme consequences called love.

Eva and I were high school sweethearts, I was the popular high school Senior she was the most sought after Junior whose Latin parents wanted us apart at all costs. After earning their citizenship, the last thing they wanted to see was their beautiful Latin daughter dating a *Prieto*. Who cares if he came from a middle-class, two-parent bungalow and a family income that had a little extra left to splurge?
I had a college chosen, tuition for two-years covered and coming off an amazing senior year. Homecoming King, voted most popular, most

likely to succeed, basically - "That Dude." Then the moment we all waited for arrived, Prom Night. That was the last date, the "good bye" that would sever the bond and set the bi-racial relationship train back on the right track. Instead, that was the night we conceived Darius. The marriage was insisted as a compromise to not spread the shame any further. Did I love my wife...? We were young; we were in love and full of selfishness. She couldn't live without me and I couldn't live with myself leaving her. We named him Darius because we both loved the movie *Love Jones* and thought Darius Lovehall was the smoothest brother on the planet. She packed her things after we said our "I do's" and headed off with me to Lincoln Harris University. I was changing diapers between first and third period, learning how to balance financial aid with child care and exams in summer school; until I ran into Desire at a freshman rush party. She was a determined recent grad with a "take no" from any one answer as fuel to succeed.

"You married?"
She asked seductively, obviously seeing the band on my finger.

"Can't believe you're not?"

That's just how I played.
My mom always said, "That mouth of yours is going to get you in a lot of trouble one day." But I was a flirt, I talked first - thought second.

"The name is Joy, but my friends call me Desire."

"Marquel, Marq... but my friends call me Young Denzel," I joked, just to see where this was going.

"You're cute," she smiled complimenting both my wit and charm in the same breath.

It had been a while since I had a night out, some time away... a break!

"I have a business offer for you."

"You're a business woman?"

"Don't I look like one?"

She laughed again jokingly and brushed me in a way that caused my weight to shift, caused my temperature to rise slightly; turning a funny moment into a serious situation. I took her card, took a tour and realized I could keep us afloat. Pay our housing; pay the lease on the car, toys for Darius. More money meant less problems and Eva and I found a marriage balance. I got much more flexibility to study, more time to work overtime at B.A.S.I.K. with less complaining. Family trips to the aquarium, a new pocketbook or extending her gym membership a few months; it all seemed to work.

The problem was I met a lot of women. Some who touched me mentally, emotionally, psychologically and others that I led for gain, both dangerous scenarios.

So I juggled two-lives with the help of the internet. My business clients were cyber, so it made lying a bit easier.

I was a good father, so I was justified by making ends meet.

I loved my wife, so I justified it by keeping the biggest secret possible, for as long as possible.

THE LEGACY

HARLEM

"Opportunity may knock only once, but temptation leans on the doorbell." -unknown

It was a three-and-a-half-hour drive from my Parrish to the capital of Kingston. Legacy and I had made this trip countless times, so those hours flew by like mere minutes as we burned our best product for relaxation. The cool ocean breeze blowing from the Caribbean Sea matched the numbing feeling the sprinkled opium provided. We were on our way to see Dr. Bird; the man above the man. He controlled acres of un-harvested hemp deep in the jungles and the support system of our entire operation. Only a select few were given the opportunity to meet the Doctor, so this trip was even more special at a young age. I was only thirteen and my reputation had spread across the island like a brush fire. He personally requested my presence at his notorious mansion on the hill so I sat in the passenger seat of Legacy's car thinking about the meeting.

The sugarcane fields surrounding his mansion were unlike anything I'd ever seen. They stood like guards protecting the narcotic fortress that sat in the middle of nowhere. It was late afternoon by the time Legacy and I arrived at the home of Dr. Bird. His mansion was protected in the same manner the Secret Service protected the White House. The scent of exotic hemp lingered in the air as we entered the front door. Gunmen guarded every corner of his sanctuary with exotic guns and excessive Fort Knox safety measures that only heightened my intimidation.

"Legacy wah gwan," Dr. Bird announced excited to see us.

He was nothing like I'd imagined. He looked young in appearance but his locks revealed his true age. The darkness of his fingers and lips meant he'd been smoking his life away for years. Beautiful half-naked women surrounded him like peasants did Pharaoh's and the sight of black nipples and well proportioned breast revealed my true age as I stood captivated by the nudity.

"This mus be da lickle youth?"

"Harlem," I mustered the courage to say.

It's amazing how meeting someone of power and prestige could be intimidating. My childhood evolved into rubbing shoulders with killers and grown men twice my age. I had somehow grown and matured much faster than average teenagers my age.

"Little Dread," he shouted, giving me a big hug.

Just like that I was initiated into the drug empire, a place with no rules or morality.

**

The mesmerizing dance of smoke rising from a lavender rose incense filled the room with a relaxing aroma. The two African wood carvings standing on both sides of my cultivation table guarded me as I worked, like gargoyles protecting a high-rise building. The soothing sounds of Sanchez flowing from my stereo and the half-smoked blunt in the ashtray were my only motivation as I worked on an unheard of strain for the Regency Fair. A rubber band held my locks from my face as I experimented with various female seeds and tested new growing nutrients. I was fully aware of the end result of this project but getting there was going to be a different story. I'd completely converted the back room of my tiny apartment into a small-scale grow-op and the faint green light of my desk lamp was the only light that illuminated the room. The irritating sound of my telephone ringing broke my concentration.

"Harlem!" I answered a bit agitated.

"Harlem, it's Allure, we need to talk. Can you meet me at the spot?"

I met Allure during my freshmen year at Lincoln Harris. Her skin was the color of Palmers Cocoa butter and depending on the time of day and the amount of lighting, she could pass for Caucasian or Black. Something about her was intriguing; the way she walked and talked was like poetry in motion. Her good looks and her female entourage made it easier for her to collect police intel. The son of the police chief was her best friend's girl, her cousin was the admin to the head of the DEA and two members of her team dated APD cops, so our infiltration of the police department ran deep. We met at our campus cafeteria which sat just between the gymnasium and library. This was our regular conversation location since the constant traffic and noise made it perfect for drowning out our classified business.

"Harlem, we got a slight problem.' Allure opened up, cutting straight to the point.

"Faze and his boys robbed Squeeze yesterday, I think he was trying to send us a message."

"Jesus! Is he ok? How much did this set us back?"

"He only had about $3,000 worth of work on him. He's in the hospital right now but says Faze asked him to pass on a message."

"Round up the team and meet me at the hospital in an hour."

Today was a different type of meeting for the Empire. Instead of meeting to discuss money or our success for the month, we stood surrounding Squeeze as he lay unconscious in the hospital bed. The constant beeping of the heart monitor was the only sound filling the room as we stood amazed at how bad he looked.

"See Harlem, I told you we should have dealt with them that night downtown," Felony spoke up.

"The doctor said he might be out for a while since they drugged him up pretty good to numb the pain," 20/20 chimed in shaking his head in disbelief.

"I say we round up the goons and show these bout it' bout it' fools how we get down?" Messiah said adding his two cents.

"That's exactly what they want us to do," I responded to Messiah who was a few seconds from punching a hole in the wall.

"What we have to do is wait for the right time to strike back," Allure said holding Squeeze's hand.

"If he comes after me with that garbage, I'm laying them down quite flat," Shaa' proclaimed pulling a glock-nine from his waist line.

"Put that away!" Cardinal whispered. "We already got a lot of heat on us; a murder would only add gasoline to the fire."

"Listen, This is what happens when we step outside of the business plan we have laid out. We never do outside deals without going through the proper channels."
My statement caused them all to hang their heads in shame knowing they'd all made side deals once or twice in their time.

"Let's be more aware of what's going on, it's obvious that Faze is doing his best to infiltrate our camp, let's not give him the opportunity."
We all stood in silence watching our fallen comrade. Allure flinched as she felt Squeeze wiggle his fingers.

"Squeeze, baby! I think he's coming around yall!"
We all huddled around the bed waiting for some clues, some reasons, some answers.

"What's good yall?" Squeeze whispered.

"What up man," we all responded.

"It was a set-up, I got a call asking for some weight and when I showed up Faze and his boys were waiting."

"That's some bitchassness!" Messiah screamed out.

"Im'ma be I'ight though, yall don't worry about me, as soon as I get better Im'ma be back getting this money."
We all broke out in laugher, by his comment.

"Why don't we clear out and give you some space," I suggested.

"We need you to rest up and get better," Allure chimed in giving him a kiss on the cheek.

"Damn, I'm feeling a little sick," Felony chimed in. "Can I get a kiss like that too?" His comment caused us all to break out in laugher again.

"Shut up!" Allure slapped him as we all headed towards the exit.

"Harlem," Squeeze called for me before I could reach the exit.

"Wsup man?" I asked leaning in close.

"I overheard one more thing before I blacked out."

I listened carefully as his voice expressed concern and urgency.

"Faze is a bigger problem than we thought!"

PURSUIT OF INTEREST

QUINTIN

I find bits and pieces of you in the music I love.

My cornrows were unbraided and out in a large unmanageable afro. Nia took every opportunity to remind me that I looked like that character from the cartoon *The Boondocks*. I'd just finished another long day of lectures and studying so the last place I wanted to be was at work trying to dodge Dr. Newman. I hid in Nia's room trying to discover more about my mysterious art teacher.

"Are you going to let me braid that thing on your head," Nia asked sarcastically looking over her lesson plans.

"You going to help me wash it and all that?"

"Please, let Dr. Newman see you. You would be begging me for some doo-doo braids."

"You got jokes," I laughed taking a seat on her desk.

"So art is your thing, huh?"

"So music is yours?" she shot back.

Typical New Yorker, I thought.

"They say art and music are one in the same."

Impressed by her statement I listened closely.

"In some ways the two help strengthen the marriage between the left and right sides of our brains."

"Heavy..." was all I could muster up as a response.

She blushed as I stared at her in amazement.

"So what kind of music do you like anyway?" I questioned. "Probably Beyoncè, you on your *Bow Down* tip, huh?"

She laughed again.

"I love B, don't get it twisted, but I prefer *Eric B. Is President* the bass line on that track, insane."

I picked my jaw up off the floor with her response.

"What do you know about hip hop, Ms?"

"Excuse me, I'm from Brooklyn Boo," She responded with that up North swag I missed.

I smiled at her comment and shot back some trivia.

"Ok Ms. Brooklyn, then you know a little something about the "backpack" era?"

"You mean like Black Moon, De La Soul and the entire Native Tongue Movement?"

She was starting to catch on to my questioning and threw a jab.

"You must have been rooting for Nas during the *"Ether"* beef, Queens boy."

"Dag, you hit below the belt Ma'"

"I'ight, name two hot tracks from '89?" I quizzed her again.

"*Children's Story*, by Slick Rick and *Fight the Power*, Public Enemy."

"Give me two from the 90's," she shot back.

"That's easy, *Bonita Applebum*, A Tribe Called Quest and *Looking at the Front Door*, Main Source."

We kept going back-and-forth naming all we could from each year.

"'91 and '92 were dope," we joked.

"Yea Naughty by Nature's *OPP*, Fresh Prince and Jazzy Jeff with *Summertime*, Digital Underground had *Same Song*, Gangstarr dropped *DWYCK*, Pete Rock and C.L. Smooth killed it with *T.R.O.Y and* Leaders of the New School linked up with Tribe called Quest for *Scenario!*" We both shouted.

The room grew silent and we stared at each other in amazement.

"Listen, would you be interested in grabbing a bite to eat after work one night? I mean we could talk more about art and music if you'd like."

"I'd like that, just promise you'll get that hair braided, first."

***

The intensity at the table was thick. The seven pieces in my hand were decent, but I sized up my opponents to get a better feel for a possible positive outcome. The pot was an easy $5,000 and my left over financial aid money was my buy-in. The clown across from me wore dark shades like we were in a World Series of Poker Tournament; little did he know his glasses acted like mirrors and I could easily see his pieces. The older gentlemen to my left seemed like an aged vet; kept his pieces close to his chest and showed no expression. But knowing my pieces and the idiot across from me gave me the advantage once the first domino was laid down. The quiet sister sitting to my right led putting down her double-twelve and looking to me for the next play - advantage her.

Intentions was quiet in the middle of the day. Only a handful of people cluttered the tables above the nightclub that buzzed with mellow music coming from the speakers and the sounds of preparation for this evening's crowd below. Dee sat by the door guarding the atmosphere and the money. The black safe behind the counter was only opened when your buy-in was approved and payouts needed to be made. Today he sat with his feet elevated reading a Rosa Acosta *SHOW* magazine issue with a devilish grin across his face. My mind drifted between the game and thoughts of Nia and my ex Spelling. The similarities and differences were striking. I missed Spelling like I missed the rudeness of New Yorkers, the harshness of the city winters and the complex grid of the streets that dissected every borough. Everything about the South was different, the music, the clothing and even the women. The ladies down South seemed to be so over developed, or as Caesar would call it, "thick." I can't lie I enjoyed watching the reaction T.I. and Lil Wayne records had on the exceptionally thick ones but tri-state sister's possessed street wit blended with street fashion; a deadly combination for a generation built on impression and reputation. But Nia, reminded me of New Year's Eve in Time Square, the thrill of game night at Madison Square Garden and rooftop nights in the summer. Spelling and I were forever bound by experience. The tattoo of the "Q" over her heart was a symbol that I was forever marked on her soul. She was a large part of my past, how my love for dominos and music were forever fused together.

"Your move young blood," the older player reminded me, breaking my daydream.

I analyzed the pieces in front of me laid out in an unusual pattern. From the looks of what was played and what I was still holding, I could tell I had the upper hand.

"I laid a piece that I knew would tilt the odds in my favor.

"Wrap," the player to my left announced, meaning he had no moves to make.

"Damn, wrap." the player next to him sat back frustrated as well.

I watched the sister next to me analyze her hand and look at me with slight confusion. This hand was similar to a game I remember Spelling and I playing one night. She was able to lock me in because I started thinking offensive, I was only thinking of going for the kill. When the hand required you to play defense and lure your opponent in. The female player to my right possessed that same look in her eye. She was eyeing the jackpot; she saw red and wanted to go for the kill. She laid her piece with certainty and conviction and stared at me for a reaction. I quietly laid my next piece knowing that the other two players were no longer factors.

"Jesus!" both players mumbled frustrated that the jackpot we all had our eyes on was slipping from their grasp.

She played her next piece and smiled realizing we only had two dominoes remaining. Her excitement caused her to miss the fact that I only had her playing one side of the board; she was oblivious that I was playing her right into a corner.

Wham!

She slammed her next piece with the taste of the jackpot on her tongue. Once again I quietly laid my piece waiting for her to come back to reality. The two players that had become spectators braced knowing what was about to happen, they both laid down pieces knowing they no longer had a chance in the game. Their two pieces sent her into panic mode. She searched her reaming piece over the board a couple times hoping the dots would change in her favor. Before she could say a word I laid my final piece down. The entire table went silent. This was how Spelling groomed me to play, this was how money was made, and this was another jackpot for the Bennet family.

Touch Of Expectation

Marquel

"You love the first person that emotionally touches you and never love anyone quite that way again." - unknown

The first time I touched a woman that wasn't my wife I was nervous; the smoothness of their skin, the contoured angles and erotic aura of femininity. The majority of women that came to Body Language didn't want sex, they wanted romance. They wanted to be desired without judgment, they wanted happiness without pressure and we all had our different methods of achieving that.

This was how I met the Mayor, Denim and Zae', three guys that would eventually show me the true power of persuasion.

"Mayor this is Marquel, Marquel this is the Mayor," Desire introduced.

"What's good young blood?" Mayor asked.

His hand shake firm and strong like his jaw line.

"Welcome to Body Language," he stated with a devilish grin.

"Marquel is going to be working with us, so I'm counting on you and the fella's to show him how things work."

"Marquel," he repeated walking around me in observation.

"He's kind of young don't you think?"

Desire walked over to me and smiled. I'll never forget that smile. It was a smile that made me feel both manly and worthless in the same emotion.

"We'll call him Young Denzel," she proclaimed.

"Young Denzel," the Mayor chuckled.

Her touch filling his eyes with jealousy and hate.

"Do you know what we do here at Body Language?" Desire asked.

"The sign outside says massage parlor, so I have an idea."

My statement caused them both to snicker under their breath.

"That's right Young Denzel and that's the answer we always want to hear." This time she brushed my chin softly and leaned into me seductively.

"I'll be giving you your pre-orientation personally."

She quickly exited the room leaving the Mayor and I in a battle of testosterone. I cleared my throat and looked around the lobby.

"Nice place you guys got here."

From his lack of response I could tell we had gotten off on the wrong foot. The sound of the front door opening broke the awkward silence.

"Mayor! What's good baby?" Denim shouted as he entered the lobby.

"Who's the young guy?" Zae' asked.

"Gentlemen meet Young Denzel, Young D this is Denim and Zae' your new co-workers."

"Wsup fella's?"

"Welcome to the team," Zae' announced breaking the silence between us.

I would later come to find out that The Mayor was Desires top dollar staff member. Their off-again on-again relationship was driven by business and pleasure, both knowing how to separate the two.

"Let's show you the place," Denim announced.

His suggestion sending the three of us off to check out the rooms, leaving Mayor in the lobby pissed in silence.

As my popularity and clientele grew, I would quickly learn the hierarchy of dominance at Body Language.

***

Desire's crib was disgustingly big. She lived in the posh district of Buckhead where money and reputation went hand in hand. The mint-green Range Rover and S-Class Mercedes in her driveway meant things at Body Language were going exceptionally well. I rang her doorbell nervous and anxious to get my orientation underway. Desire opened her door and greeted me in a Fredrick's of Hollywood uniform that would embarrass the Playboy staff. Noticing my surprise, she pulled me inside to avoid nosey neighbors and desperate housewife gossip.

"Did I catch you at a bad time?"

"Bad time...Young Denzel you're just in time."

"I don't understand, I thought this was going to be my orientation?"

"It is sweetheart, so calm down and relax."

She headed off to another room and left me admiring her home in amazement.

"Come join me in my office." she yelled from a back room.

Her office was big and spacious. I took a seat in front of her large mahogany desk as she poured me a drink to calm the edge.

"Let's get down to business shall we? We work on a client based system at Body Language which means the more ladies you see the more money you make. We have a 75 – 25 pay scale, which means 75% of your profit is mine and you walk away with the other 25% so I strongly encourage going that extra mile for tips."

Back then her comment seemed comical but over time I made more money on tips than that measly 25% kick back Body Language offered. I discovered erogenous zones some women never knew existed; their exposed clavicle bone, the delicate center of their palms and if I really needed a big tip, the sensitive soles of their feet.

"Listen Young Denzel you work for me now," she proclaimed making her way to my side of the desk.

I quickly swallowed the last of the contents in my cup to hide my obvious attraction to my employer.

"The second part of your orientation will be a hands-on course for evaluation," she explained. "It's important that I fully prepare you for your new position."

***

"Hello caller you're on the air!"

"Marquel my main man, what it do?"

"Can't call it but I'm listening, you got a question or a problem?"

"Yea, my girl left me because my boy posted some pictures of me and this chick from the club on my Facebook."

"Caller, what's your name because I've got to get to the bottom of this?"

"They call me Poster."

"Well Poster, Facebook is now the biggest drug in America. You certainly aren't the first brother to get caught on Facebook and you definitely won't be the last. My advice is let her go, matter of fact you're on the perfect platform to find a new chick in no time so pull that Facebook needle out your vein cause you've officially overdosed."

"Next caller you're on the air!"

"Hey Marquel," a soft voice crooned on the other end.
"Hey sweetheart, you got a question or a problem?"
"I have a big date tonight and need a man's opinion on a very important question."
"Well I'm all ears so take your time."
"G-string or a thong?"
"Well how long have you known him?" I asked, causing Chaz and I to laugh in the background.
"We've been dating for a few weeks now and I think it's time to let him sample my goodies."
"I think the real question here is satin or lace, cause honestly once he see's either he's not going to care if it's a string or a thong. My advice is neither, if you know you're going to break him off why not save both of you some time and give him easy access."
Chaz punched some buttons on the console creating a round of applause.
"Please remember to wrap it up because he may not be worth a trip to the clinic later."

"Let's take one more caller."

"Caller you're on the air!"

"Hey Young Denzel," another soft voice whispered.

Hearing my work name being promoted over the air, caught me off guard.

"The names Marquel caller, do you have a question or a problem?"

"What does a sister have to do to get an appointment with you?"

I instantly looked at Chaz on the sound boards for some clarification. I'd always done my best to separate my personal life from my business career, so hearing her question was shocking.

"Caller I'm not sure what you're asking."

"Word is you're the best at what you do; a few ladies at my hairdresser say the guys at that massage parlor really know how to please a woman."

I put my hand over the mic to get some answers from Chaz.

"Who the hell is this?"

"They didn't leave a name."

The biggest problem was B.A.S.I.K was being syndicated in six major markets and her comment was not only incriminating me, it was raising red flags about my place of employment.

"Stay under the radar," Desire would always tell us. "Our success is based on our clientele's understanding of how

limitless and confidential our services
are."

The big problem was this secret was now
broadcasted live over the airwaves.

THE MEANS JUSTIFIES THE ENDS

CAESAR

Learn the rules so you know how to break them properly.

The sweet taste of freedom was the only thing on my mind as I pushed opened the door to a lobby filled with reporters and cameras. Coach had announced that LAHU basketball team's first practice would be closed to the media, so this paparazzi frenzy was a result of anxious reports who couldn't wait until the official press conference later.

"Mr. Bennet, how does it feel to have the responsibility of leading the number one team in the nation?" some lady asked shoving her recorder in my face.

"Well I've been playing ball all my life and I plan on approaching it as if it was just another day in the park," I responded trying to fight my way out of the mob. But the faster I walked the faster they followed.

"Mr. Bennet, how are you handling being a full time student, balancing friends and a personal life while being in the spotlight?" A short chubby guy asked nearly tripping over a crack in the sidewalk.

"It's tough being a superstar period. It makes it rough when everything you say and do is analyzed and valued in such high regard."

I was really picking up my stride now that the gym was only a few feet from the trailing cameras.

"Mr. Bennet, Mr. Bennet, one more question!" a voice screamed from the back as I pulled opened the door to the gym.

"Can you address rumors about your alleged meeting with Charles Patten a notoriously corrupt Sports Agent?"

The group of reporters suddenly fell quiet and all the tape recorders and cameras seemed to be pointing directly at my face.

"I was unaware of those allegations," I spoke up. "But I can assure you that they are completely untrue." I commented and closed the entrance of the arena behind me.

***

"How nice of you to join us Mr. Gibson!" Coach Newton yelled after blowing his whistle to get everyone's attention.

"Sorry I'm late coach."

"Save it Gibson," he yelled. "Give me five laps after you get out the training room."

I clutched my gym bag in anger and headed towards the locker room.

I was back on court where the team had already gathered in a circle at half court.

"Alright, listen up guys," Coach said. "We have our opening game vs. UCLA in a few weeks; there are a few things I want to adjust in our playbook to be ready for game day, does everyone understand?"

We all nodded our heads in agreement.

"Let's get "teamwork in on three" he said enthusiastically.

Everyone got in tight and joined hands in the center.

"Teamwork on three….teamwork on three…1…2….3…teamwork!" we all shouted together in unison.

Everyone got in lay-up lines for warm ups, while Coach Newton called me over.

"Listen here Gibson, you're my star point guard," he whispered. "I need you to be the leader, the guys believe in you, they look up to you. I'm counting on your leadership to take us to the championship again this year." Putting his arm on my shoulder and guiding me to the opposite end of the court.

"Showing up late for practice is setting a bad example, and I want to make sure you're ready for the responsibility of carrying this team."

"I'm sorry coach, about being late, it won't happen again."

"Meet me in my office after practice so we can talk more," he said. He turned back to the team clapping and yelling instructions.

"I need Gibson, Merchant, Davis, Brown and Phillips out, the rest of you on the sidelines," Coach instructed.

As I heard Coach call out my name I thought back to the days when I first picked up a basketball. My father would take me to watch games at the Staples Center. I admired Kobe as he brought the ball up the court with grace and skill. The other four players followed his lead like the conductor in the Harlem choir. I watched as he pushed the ball up, go behind the back and dish it off to the wingman for an easy two. I told my father, "I'm going to be just like Kobe...just wait and see," he would laugh and rub me on the head. At the end of my senior year, I had racked up more trophies than the law would allow. It all meant nothing to the animosity and betrayal I felt when my father walked out on us. Leaving my mother and I with bills and loans to pay back on a house that was twice her salary. I watched her work two jobs just to make the mortgage payment and left her little or no time for herself. Finally, when she had enough, we packed what we could sold the house and moved in with my aunt Joyce in Atlanta.

When I have that basketball in my hands I think back to Staples Center. I remember my father's laugh, and his doubt of me being a leader. Every pass on the mark, every jump shot perfect, not to make him proud but to replace the hurt and loneliness he gave my mother and I.

A leader just like Kobe, I told you Dad; just like Kobe.

Reap the Harvest

Harlem

"People don't buy what you do; they buy why you're doing it." - unknown

The air had a certain aroma when you stepped off the plane. Legacy flew the entire Empire back home to celebrate what Dr. Bird called a "momentous occasion." It was Jamaica's 50th independence so this visit was going to be slightly more special than all the others. Since this was my little brother Arius' senior year of high school, I decided to bring him along for the memorable trip.

> "I'm glad to be out of Atlanta," Allure expressed fitting in with her island flare.
>
> "I haven't been home since I was a little boy," I overheard Arius tell her, helping her with her bag.

Dancehall music had started its ascent up the music charts and its popularity was earning the genre regular spins on top radio stations. This made what we were doing relevant, current and cool. The success of The Empire gave us the freedom to make regular trips like this back home. Our usual trips led us to Spanish Town Road for *Passa Passa*, the biggest dancehall gathering in the world. Locals would string out sound systems bigger than some of the shanties and shut down the entire block. This was the source of our inspiration; the fancy footwork and badman movements. Flames shot into the air like dragon's taking deep breaths with the help of hairspray and lighter fluid. Blow horns screamed every time the selector spun a wicked tune and pulled it back to hear the crowd's reaction.

"Why do you think Dr. Bird wants us all here?" Messiah questioned, taking his bag from the carousel.

"Who cares?" Cardinal chimed in. "We are going to party!"

"Preach," Squeeze agreed with a noticeable limp and his hand in a brace.

"Who knows, but we have to remain quiet about our plans to part ways with his business plan."

"They better not try anything," Felony urged as we all headed out to find our ground transportation.

We were on Legacy's turf which meant we were treated like royalty; some real Coming to America material. A handful of Mercedes Benz Sprinters waited curbside to take us directly to Dr. Bird's mansion in style. The last time I took this trip I was a teenager and was embraced into this fast money lifestyle. The weekend would be filled with blunts the size of expensive Cuban cigars and evenings sleeping on waterbeds filled with Appleton rum. Arius loved the V.I.P. perks the island offered and I hated that he envied the person I became.

"My American Comrades," Dr. Bird announced in his thickest Patwa accent.
We all sat at attention still hung over from a week filled with sex, partying and drugs. The big announcement was Dr. Bird was transferring his power over to Legacy and naming him his successor. The decision had major implications with the rival top dealers who felt they were more deserving. But on this one night, there would be no violence. There would be no arguments. Tonight was the changing of the guards.

***

The stakes were much higher now that the reckless cartels in Mexico made the headlines nightly, news stations flaunted the success of the governments new drug initiatives. Under Legacy's reign, my job was now to make sure that eighty percent of our monthly profits were accurate and delivered on time. That was far greater than the original cut we were given. This only made my decision to leave easier.

A large percent of our profits came from Marijuana so my first plan was to break my dependency on Legacy and grow my own product. Long gone were the days of digital scales, clumsy plastic sandwich bags and secret exchange locations. We were the twenty-first century distributors and learned to adapt to the changing climate. Not only did we sell it, we found a way to help consumers enjoy it without the fear of the law. Hookah bars did it, Cigar shops allowed it, so we created members only relaxation locations. The process didn't take force, big body guards or manpower to implicate. It started with a membership process that required valid approval, a background check and a simple e-mail confirmation. Membership was usually granted in 24 to 48 hours or how long it took to get the background check approved, then each day the new location would be tweeted or sent encoded via e-mail to all members of locations in their area. We rotated eight locations daily to accommodate our clientele and business doubled once membership came with occasional free perks.

What other business had such a high demand increase without a required price decrease? The 4-month cultivation process from seedling to flowering was a quick enough turn around to keep the members who just needed a "buzz" satisfied. Diverse enough to keep those who needed the "high" fulfilled and the connoisseurs who needed to stay "stoned" coming back for more. We had three different grow houses all on scattered cycles. The "Indica" grow house grew the strongest strains – Blueberry, Northern Lights... etc. Our "Sativa" grow house held the stimulant and medicinal plants while our third grew all the Hydroponic ("Hydro") strains. While campus organizations like NORML and other global groups worked to put a positive spin on the drug, the fact was the government could never wrap their arms around the growth, distribution and sale of marijuana. The $17 billion dollars spent a year on the War on drugs could be used to pay teachers what they really deserve, Firemen for risking their lives and the elderly for their social security. We all joked about making marijuana legal with restrictions, like cigarettes. You could only smoke it in designated areas, could only purchase it from designated resellers. How mellow would the world be if you could walk into 7-eleven and pick up a carton of "OG Kush" and go home and mellow out? Picture the influx of revenue our economy would receive if the grower, distributor and consumer were all taxed like tobacco users?

QUALITY VS QUANTITY

QUINTIN

Music is what feelings sound like...

Adolescence up North meant having to learn quick, you had to adapt. I guess that was a quality all city kids possessed. The suburbs did something to you. Like when Spike Lee's character *Lady Bug* went to stay with her aunt down south in the movie *Crooklyn*. You could see the stars, you could hear the crickets, and people actually acknowledged each other. The same thing applied to the music. There was a huge difference between Jay-Z and T.I., a tremendous gap between Skyzoo and Lil Wayne and a million-and-one light-years between De La Soul and 2 Live Crew. If there was one person who could balance on that bridge it would be Nia.

I worked frantically to clean my place before Nia arrived. I guess you could call this our first date but I wanted to make my first impression my best. She should be here any minute and insisted she drive us to dinner, her clever way of checking my place out.

The doorbell to my tiny 2-bedroom apartment rang causing the butterflies in my stomach to flutter. I stood on the opposite side of the door building up the nerve to impress.

"Wsup Nia?"

"Wsup Q?"

We both laughed at the seriousness of our nerves cutting the thick tension on the situation.

"Come in, come in."

"Your spot is nice," she complimented taking in my living room.

"Thank you, at least I know you have good taste."

She laughed again; it was the kind of laugh you never wanted to end. I admired her swag as she stood taking my place in. Her olive fitted cap was tucked low on her brim and her skinny jeans hugged her all the way down to her ankles. Her matching Olive IX's were tiny, a size 5 easy, and the sloppiness of her laces made me smile. I watched as she slipped her kicks off and made her way in like she lived there.

"You don't have to take your shoes off."

"It's cool, I have manners."

"If you had manners you wouldn't have walked out your house with those tight ass pants on."

"What these? They not tight!" she insisted poking her butt out to make sure I took her all in.

"I ain't mad."

We both laughed again at the ease of our vibe.

"You think you got enough records?" She asked thumbing through my collection.

She picked up an old Frankie Beverly and Maze record and started to sing.

"Before I let you....Gooooo!"

I admired her as she made herself at home rummaging through all my stuff.

"What size fitted you wear? 7 − 7 ½?" she asked making her way to my hats.

"Yea, how you guessed?"

"Please with that big ol' head of yours."

"You got jokes."

"Let me see what size you wear?" I demanded snatching her fitted off.

"You're cold blooded, you wear the same size as me," I jabbed, putting her hat on.

"Don't... I don't want you to mess up your hair," she jumped to snatch it back.

I'm not sure if she really wanted to stop me from messing up my hair or just a lame excuse to enter my personal space but we were now face to face; Close enough for our souls to dance. I took deep breaths of her inhaling fruity body mist scents. We both shared another laugh.

"So are you done checking all my stuff out?"

"Yea, just making sure you checked out."

"Can we go get something to eat now?" I quizzed.

"Sure, you're driving," She insisted throwing me the keys to her bike.

"I don't know how to drive that thing."

"What better time to learn than now."

Thankfully all those years of driving stick shift jalopies back in N.Y. made adjusting to her bike easy. I cruised downtown Atlanta with Nia's arms wrapped around my waist, the wind in our face and chemistry between our two bodies.

***

I came across a tall stocky gentleman talking to a group of young brothers near the Yard so I made my way over to see what he could be saying to garner so much attention.

"Gather around gentlemen! I am Big Brother Wholesale, the president of Nu Beta Psi National Fraternity Incorporated, Phi Theta Chapter. I am here to invite you to our interest meeting in a few weeks!" He screamed, handing out fliers.

"Quintin, right," Big Brother Wholesale asked extending his hand.

"Yea," I replied shaking his hand nonchalantly.

"You know my brothers and I have heard a lot of great things about you, your reputation at *Intentions* makes you a very important person to know. This domino competition thing you have going is really creating a buzz around Atlanta."

"Really?" I responded nonchalantly not knowing exactly how popular Dee and I were becoming.

"We here at Nu Beta Psi have always had an interest in you becoming a brother in our organization."

"I never understood the benefit of joining a fraternity," I said puzzled.

"Because you are a brother with ambitions and goals. That's the type of people we are looking for to lead our organization into the 21st century, not to mention our sister sorority with well over 55 active, smart, beautiful and willing members. Here's my number, give me a call if you're ever interested in the direction of your future," he said handing me a card and disappearing into the crowd of people that began to fill the Yard.

The push for popularity was amusing so I watched the Freshmen frenzy for a few minutes before heading off for my next class.

GENERATION - Y - NOT

MARQUEL

"The internet is becoming the town square for the global village of tomorrow" – Bill Gates

I was pissed my DVR hadn't recorded my favorite show. I almost forgot what life was like before the ability to pause, stop and rewind live TV. I'm sure it was similar to archaic methods of winding a car window up by hand, unraveling yourself from a telephone cord or trying to find a stamp to mail a letter. I found myself right in the center of two generational societies. My childhood was filled with 56K dial up modems that sang, whistled and blocked your phone line from accepting important calls. Big bulky cell phones displayed black numerical digits on the tiny green screen and too large to carry in your pocket. Now, my son Darius streamed his cartoons directly to his iPad, I could access the internet anytime/anywhere or turn into another person on social networks and expand my client base in the Atlanta Metro area.

Here I was, living on the equator of old school and the generational shift of the new. A new world of isolation behind faceless chat boards and blogging websites; the new millennia gave us instant broadband results, cut & paste creativity and the end of face-to-face interaction and patience. Many of my clients followed my every move on *Twitter*, used the internet super highway to book their appointments and sometimes solicited my talents on *Craigslist* when Body Language would not accommodate my regulars. With all the benefits that followed the dominance of the *World Wide Web*, a gradual shift in the future began. Kids my son's age became techies and spoke textese (LOL, SMH, OMG) before they learned to write their alphabets. Cell phones, computers and GPS systems all became new forms of life support, while the development of the human brain took a back seat. In the end I could never find a website or Facebook wall that would help me pass my three-o'clock Literature exam, never discovered a chat board that would boost my GPA or guarantee a comfortable five-figure salary and job security.

The weekend was right around the corner which ment I'd have to spend some time with Abigail before she started popping up unexpectedly.

Despite Abigail's annoying persistence, her connections to the city made her a prized commodity. Dope boys, club promoters and famous local artists knew her by name. Her umbilical cord to the Atlanta streets was never cut and the state of Georgia nurtured her into an irresistible Peach.

As rough as she seemed to the world, Abigail was as soft as a marshmallow when we were together. She was a hopeless romantic and the dirt bag brothers she attracted knew nothing about sweeping her off her feet. She loved the artist *KEM* so I made sure I had his station cued on Pandora. It was a Wednesday which meant she was coming straight from boot camp and could use some extra pampering. This was me "going the extra mile." Even covered in sweat and exhausted she still walked into Body Language looking stunning.

"How was your day sweetheart?"

"Don't sweetheart me," she responded letting her Southern Hospitality shine bright.

"How was Boot Camp?"

"Marquel, I'm not in the mood today, I just want to be broken off properly so I can go home and get some sleep."

I smiled at her comment and opened the door with an even better plan in store. The scent of amaretto scented oils greeted her entrance and I could see her armor of difficulty crumbling before me.

"What's all this?"

"What?" I responded playing dumb.

I took her hand and ushered her in the rest of the way.

"Why don't you take this," I encouraged, handing her a robe and leading her to the soaker tub I had drawn filled with bubbles.

To my surprise she didn't even question me and did as I asked. I walked over and hit play on the *BOSE* speaker in the corner and the sultry sounds of KEM filled the room. Her deep sigh signaled it was time for me get her favorite Sushi I had delivered prepped and plated. I poured two glasses of Moscato wine and walked one glass back to the tub with some slippers.

"What are you doing to me?" she asked, eyes closed and drifting off into bliss.

"For you," I smiled handing her the wine and placing the slippers just outside the tub.

"How was your day?"

She gave me that crazy look, like I had just asked her to commit one of the seven deadly sins, but the secure feelings of my hands kneading the day's stress from her back and shoulders caused her to confess.

"This producer tried to stiff me out of my payment for a video I was in."

"Umm hum," I acknowledged knowing there was more.

"We had to catalog and finish the inventory on all the new books at the book store."

"What?" I responded to reassure her I was still listening.

"And then we spent half of our Boot Camp running and doing burpees."

"That's insane," I commented opening the drain to empty the tub.

"Don't tell me my time is up?"

"Of course not, I have dinner waiting."

"Dinner?" She questioned as I wiped her down softly with a towel.

The glow of her skin mixed with the soft lighting and the flicker of the candles made the level of temptation escalate. I took my button-up off and put it on her knowing the scent of me drove her crazy. I stopped by Vicki's earlier that day and picked her up a pair of boy shorts in her size. I made sure I popped the tag on them to ease her fears of them being some other woman's panties. I took her hand and led her over to the table and pulled her chair out.

"Why do you have to be married?" she questioned taking another sip of her wine and admiring all her favorite rolls on display.

"I don't want to ruin our time talking about "what if's" let's just enjoy the time we have right now," I commanded.

It was a trick I picked up from Desire. No one likes being told what to do, but if asked with the right balance of intensity and security it could drive you crazy.

I watched as Abigail shifted her weight slightly turned on.

We talked; we talked about everything, laughed, and connected. I gave Abigail more than a quick orgasm, I made love to her mind, her heart, her soul and when our hour-and-a-half session was over I held her hand and escorted her out the room. She left a new woman, she left fulfilled and even more in love with me than I could have ever expected.

NEW RETRO

CAESAR

"Got more kicks than a baby in a mothers stomach." - Nas

The stainless-steel briefcase sat hidden behind a stack of black and grey Jordan boxes in the corner. Sneaker boxes lined my dorm room from floor to ceiling like some obsessive wallpaper. I slid aside a stack of kicks to revisit the mysterious case I'd received weeks ago. My third pair of Space Jam XI's where tangled between the wires of my PS4 console and my freshman jersey draped over the enormous 70" flat screen. I unlocked the briefcase to reveal two limited pairs of *Air Yeezy II* surrounded by stacks of money. The Kanye West collab sneaker was $245 retail on release day but was now $6,000 resale and Patten had just given me two different colorways. *Patten sure knew how to spark my interest.* As a sneaker connoisseur this was a top 5 must have for my collection. The landscape of basketball and the sneakers we rocked had evolved. Rappers now sold more sneakers than actual ball players, kids collected and traded sneakers like basketball cards and a reselling epidemic made obtaining wide-spread general releases harder than ever. My generation became bigger and faster, many of us were ready to jump straight from high school to the big stage, but the commissioner's mandatory 1-year of college rule only slowed down the flood of young talent. The fact was some of us were still kids in the body of grown men. Product endorsements alone paid more than nine-to-five salaries? Kids who never saw real money could now turn their hobbies and fantasies into reality. My addiction was sneakers. More than spray paint and fast women the niche market of Sole Collecting was my thing. There is no argument that the sneaker industry became famous because of the legend Michael Jordan. But that was a different time, a different era. The sneaker that turned my love into an addiction was the *Lebron II*.

The year was 2004 and the *Air Jordan* line was reaching the end of its supremacy, sneaker fans were curious which player would have the same allure. Sure Melo, Chris Paul and Derick Rose were big name replacements, but their sneakers had yet to build the same amount of hype and street cred that *Jordan I - XIV* garnered. The *Lebron I* didn't shake up the world, but the fact that King James became the Rookie of the year, won an Olympic gold Medal with Dream Team II and broke every sensible rookie record, opened the door for the *Lebron II* in 05'. This shoe opened the flood gates for something other than a Jordan Retro. Let's face it, the Jordan Retro was legendary but sneakers had to evolve like the game did and players like Lebron, Kobe and Durant generated a new buzz for sneaker and basketball enthusiasts.

***

My custom ID *Lebron X's* on my feet matched perfectly with the basketball shorts and coordinating polo. A new pair of Retro's dropped Saturday which meant I needed to secure a third pair for my collection. It was Wednesday and that meant a shipment had already arrived in stores just in time for the anticipated release in three days.

"Nice to see you could make it Caesar," Crystal announced as a mob of fans followed me into the store.

"Looks like you brought your fan club too?" she joked.

I smiled sarcastically, trying my best to sign every recite, business card or strange item people could find for me to sign. A line of regular Sneakerheads had already begun to form at the front of the store in anticipation for the big weekend release.

"Alright ladies and gentlemen, shows over!" mall security shouted, trying to calm down the growing frenzy.

"I hit you up a few weeks ago, when the *KD IV's* came in," Crystal reminded me with a smile and a wink.

Truth was, I usually received two or three pairs of each shoe directly from their corporate headquarters weeks before the release. Since our team was the best in the nation, the television coverage and media attention I received meant instant sales for whoever I decided to endorse that day. But the *Carmine VI* was going to be big. So big that I was only sent one pair which wasn't going to suffice. I still needed a pair to put on ice and a pair for my outrageous collection back in my dorm room.

"My bad Crystal, you know how things get with midterms on the horizon?"

"So you're coming to get the *VI's*?"

"Yea, did you already get your shipment in?"

"Do you see that line outside the store? We definitely got them."

"Follow me, I have a place that you can try them on in peace."

The stockroom of a sneaker store is every sneaker enthusiast wet dream. Rows of sneakers stacked ceiling high in multiple bins formed a Fort Knox of sneaker inventory. Orange colored Nike boxes sat next to black Jordan boxes. *Reebok, Adidas, New Balance, Asics, Converse* and even *Vans* sneakers all sat in harmony unaware of the battle for footwear domination.

"They're right back here; we haven't even taken them out the boxes."

I followed Crystal through the maze of bins and boxes to a room towards the back of the building. I watched as she pressed some buttons on the door combination lock to reveal a secure room. The room was filled with boxes of all shapes, a closer inspection of the labels described kicks that weren't even due out for a few months.

"Ahh, here they are."

I watched as she seductively bent over to retrieve two Jordan boxes that were set aside.

"Size 11 right? I put them aside because I knew you'd come for these."

She smiled and adjusted her already tight form fitting uniform. The *Concord XI's* on her feet arched up her tight black yoga pants and the wildness of her natural hair caused me to admire her like I'd never done before.

I took a seat on a nearby box and kicked off my *Bron's* trying to shake my desires. Now commenced my sneaker ritual - all Sneakerheads had one. For me, I had to loosen and spread the laces and the eyelets apart before I stuck my foot in. The tight stock pre-lace had a strange way of ruining the true shape of the shoe. I then unlaced the first couple of holes because I liked my laces to hang a little when I wore them casually.

I was halfway through my ritual when I felt Crystal's arms begin to massage my shoulders. She was using just the right amount of pressure to knock down my walls of rationale. She was a married woman with two kids a husband, a house and a happy home.

"Look Crystal," I began, sighing out the tension she was kneading out of my back.

"I don't think sleeping with each other is a good idea?"

"And who says I want to sleep with you?" she said making sure I got the idea that this wouldn't be the last attempt at her offer.

I already had both pairs of *Carmine VI's* on my feet and was spiraling out of control by the time Crystal made her way to my spot.

"Just tell me how much I owe you for these kicks?" I asked, feeling her hands make their way towards my instrument.

"For the shoes nothing, for my time it will cost you this," she whispered in my ear, finally awaking my serpent from his peaceful sleep.

"Look Crystal money isn't a problem," I stuttered as she stroked him like she was reloading the pressure in a super soaker.

I stood up trying to regain my composure, shocking Crystal when I turned around with all my manhood at attention. A devilish smile spread across her face as she sized me up.

"Look Caesar, I don't want anything from you, I got married early, had kids early and just feel like I've missed out on some adventures when I was younger." she explained, cornering me in the wall.

I stumbled on my shorts which were now gathered around my ankles.

That was the last thing I heard before I felt the warmth of her mouth. I closed my eyes and thanked the sneaker game for Crystal.

***

I decided to stop by Coach Newton's office since I had time to burn between classes. I had a lot of respect for coach because he really took a chance on recruiting me. He saw something in me that UCLA and USC couldn't because I was a young kid that fell in with the wrong crowd. I remember my senior year of high school he showed up after one of my games and asked my mother if he could have a word with her. He talked her into packing up meaningless memories of my father and heading to Atlanta to be closer to my Aunts.

"Hey, Caesar," Coach said, leaning back in his big leather chair.

Coach was a tall lanky brother who used to play ball back in the '80s. Behind his desk hung trophies, plaques, newspaper clippings and autographed basketballs on shelves. Stacks of playbooks and new offenses were scattered all over his desk as he removed his glasses and pointed to the seat on the other side.

"Have a seat son, what's bothering you?"

"Nothing Coach, just had some spare time, so I decided to stop by and kick it."

"Kick it?" he replied taking a sip of his stale coffee that was sitting under some notebooks. "What is that, some new street slang?"

"Come on Coach, you have to adapt to the new lingo."

"Well what's new?"

"I'm still getting calls from persistent agent's everyday."

"Don't let those money hungry fools get in the way of why I brought you here," coach said pulling his chair closer to the desk.

"Yea I know, to win us championships, Coach."

"No, to get an education boy and don't you forget it."

"Yes sir," I replied trying not to provoke the lack of sleep that showed on his face.

"Look Caesar, kids like you only come around once in a lifetime. Do you remember when I came to your high school game to talk to your mother?"

He asked as if I could ever forget.

"You were a 5'9" point guard with no right hand, now look at you, 6'6" with a killer crossover and considered the best in the Nation. I've watched you jump seven spots in the draft since your freshman year, not to mention you're about to take our school to its third national championship. I just don't want to see you throw all of that away messing with some money grubbing agent."

"I know, I know Coach," I interrupted trying to avoid another stay-in-school lecture.

I made a promise to my mother and coach that I would stay in college and get my degree no matter how much the National Basketball Association taunted me.

"We have a very hard schedule this year Caesar," Coach continued to explain.

"The NCAA says that our two consecutive championships exhibits our schedule may be too effortless, so they have added North Carolina, Florida and Memphis to our schedule this season."

Those were the three most heavily recruited schools in the Southeast, I thought, as Coach reassured me with a quick rundown of their rosters.

"This year I plan on making you the captain of our team," Coach confessed.

"I'm going to announce it to the team when the season starts in a few weeks."

I was shocked, even though I was the best player on the team I was never put in a leadership role. Being the captain meant that both on and off the court I had to be a leader, a responsibility I was ready to acquire.

"Did you ever play for the NBA Coach?" I asked never hearing his name in any of its record books.

I watched as a cloud of darkness fell on his face. Coach sat back in his chair once again turning his chair around to face his many accolades that hung from the wall.

"Let me tell you something about the NBA, Caesar. You become a machine when you are drafted, your mind and body must always be at its prime, for fault in either can lead to banishment. I was drafted once and tore my ACL at draft camp. I was sent to the ABA and even played a few years overseas to show coaches I still had the potential, but my knee never healed right and my basketball career was short lived. That is why I became a coach, to give young brotha's like you an opportunity to fulfill a dream I could never accomplish. Caesar you have a chance to create history here at this University and I just want to be there when your dreams come true."

I watched as Coach turned his chair back around and wiped a tear that had fallen from his face. I got up and shook his hand taking another look at the wall behind him. I hoped one day I could have as many memories as Coach Newton, but for now I had class and my dreams would have to be put on hold until after Ceramics class.

EMPRESS

HARLEM

"We may have come over in different ships, but we are all in the same boat." - Whitney Young

There was still fifteen minutes of class left when I finished the last problem on Freeman's Psychology exam. I glanced at the clock on the wall and then at Marquel who was sitting two seats away to see if he was clearly as stressed as I was. It was the most punishing sixty minutes of my life, and if we hadn't prepared for this exam as early as we did, I wouldn't have even showed up to take it. I took another look at my scantron just to make sure I bubbled in all the blanks and then walked up to the front of the room to hand it in. I went back to my seat to get my bag and gave Marquel the "I gave it my best shot" look heading for the door. When I got outside I took a deep breath and waited for Marquel to finish his exam. Today was Friday and nothing was going to ruin my day. Today the Empire was going to meet for our first practice of the year. *Tropics* was only a few months away and we had to lay some foundation down for this year's show. I leaned against the wall and pulled a pack of Newport's out of my pocket, "*stressful times called for desperate measures*," I thought as I lit my cancer stick. I tried months ago to kick the habit but something stressful always lured me right back to those addictive nicotine sticks. I took a couple quick drags before Marquel opened the door and headed towards me.

"That was no joke, huh?" he said laughing

"The worst is over now," I assured him and took another pull of my cigarette.

"You know you lose a day of your life every time you spark one of those up," Marquel joked in a TRUTH commercial kind of way.

"That hasn't been proven yet," I responded, putting it out on the sole of my shoe.

"What you got planned for the rest of the day?"

"I've gotta go meet The Empire in a few."

"You guys are really making some money off that business, huh?"

"We are, but we're not meeting about business. Today is all about pleasure! We got *Tropics* in a few months and we got to get things ironed out."

"That's right, I heard ya'll were hosting it this year."

"We're going to do more than just host it, were shutting unu blood clot down."

Marquel looked puzzled as they all do when I went into my accent.

"So did you find out who your Liaison is going to be this year?"

"Liaison! What the hell are we going to need one of those for?"

"It's not a matter of needing one; you're going to be assigned one. Every student organization that will be hosting an event is assigned a Liaison to oversee the details. The last thing LAHU wants to do is get caught up in something scandalous right when we're gaining national attention."

Damn, I thought. That's exactly what The Empire and I were planning to get into - trouble.

"Well how do I find out who our Liaison will be?"

"You have to head over to the Student Union and fill out the paperwork for your event. Then they will contact you."

"I guess I'll head there now and bang that out."

"That's cool cause I got to get Darius, check me later."

I gave Marquel a pound and we headed off on our separate ways.

The Student Union was buzzing as it usually does mid-day. Beautiful sorority sisters dressed in colorful jackets and campus organizations lined the walls. It was getting close to rush season so all of LAHU's frats and sororities were out in full recruiting swing. By the time I made it to the Liaison office the arch support on my chocolate *Wallabies* began working its magic.

> "How may I help you?" a cute sister guarding the front counter asked.
>
> "Yea, I'm here to register for a Liaison to oversee our event."
>
> "Here is the paperwork you will need," she responded with a smile.

I took the rubber band off my wrists and tied my dreads back from my face. I could feel her watching me as I looked over the paperwork.

> "What kind of show will you be registering?"
>
> "*Tropics*, have you heard of it?"
>
> "Have I heard of *Tropics*?" she shouted with excitement.
>
> "I love Reggae music, PULL...UPPPP!" she screamed, forming a pistol gesture with her hands.

I smiled at her comment and grabbed a pen off her desk.

> "You look very familiar, are you Harlem...? Harlem Best, I saw you and your crew win it last year in Miami."
>
> "You did," I igged her on.

"Yall are crazy nice with the footwork, and the way you guys move your hips... turns me on."

Now this sister is talking, I thought.

"That girl yall got on your crew is wicked too! All the dudes in the crowd wanted a piece of that."

"Well we're hosting the show this year here at LAHU."

"Get out of here! Wait till I tell my home girls," she responded and picked up her phone to start dialing.

I took a seat near the entrance and started going over the questionnaire.

Last year, *Tropics* was sheer madness. All the illest dance crew's; Nice Up, MDX, G-Unit and Mighty Crown were out practicing their new moves. Allure and I would be focused on mastering the moves while the other knuckleheads would be off whining on anything with slender hips.

Once we hit the stage in Miami the crowd went insane. Women were screaming in anticipation of our set. The new riddim dropped and we all started moving in unison. The actual set was a blur but the end result was expected, we shut the show down and unanimously took home the title. It was our second straight *Tropics* victory and this year would certainly make a third.

I finished the form just in time to witness a devastating female enter the room. Her skin was the color of *V.S.O.P Hennessey* and her premature dreads were still struggling to lay flat.

"Ebony! You're back," she asked surprised.

"Yea girl, lunch is only an hour," she replied joining her behind the desk.

I approached the two of them and handed my new groupie my paperwork.

"All finished?"

"Yup, how soon will it take before we're assigned a Liaison for this event?"

"You can ask her yourself," she stated handing my paperwork to Ebony.

I watched as she read over the paperwork carefully. Her wrists adorned with ethnic shells and beads, the aroma of Mango butter soap filled my personal space. I watched the fullness of her Nubian lips, admired the way her earrings dangled from her soft lobes. The seductive arch in her eyebrows and almond color in her eyes were all works of perfection.

"Well Mr. Best, It looks like I will be the Liaison for your event."

"You can call me Harlem," I responded extending my hand to shake hers.

"Very well, then you can call me Ebony," she smiled taking in my features, just as I did hers.

"I look forward to working with you."

"So do I…" I responded making her blush.
"So do I…"

IMPROVISATIONAL

QUINTIN

"Sometimes a man finds destiny on the road he took to avoid it." - unknown

I sat anxiously on the back of Nia's *Ducati* as we cruised through campus. My *Lebron IV NYC* editions sat nestled on the foot pegs of her crotch rocket as I wrapped my arms around her waist and leaned slightly into our turn. I was already ten minutes late to my Music Lit. class, so her bike was saving me precious time as we weaved through campus traffic.

After our first date, Nia and I spent every moment possible getting to know each other. At work we were strangers but the minute we left the watchful eyes of Dr. Newman and the kids we were entwined in each other. I'd learned that Majesty and Nia used to run their block back in Brooklyn before Nia got accepted to NYU and Majesty to LAHU. Faith and time would eventually bring her and Majesty back together and renew my hopes of finding love. Before Nia, I dated off and on with some more memorable than others. There was Ayana who swam for LAHU swim team, but reminded me of those Tom-Tom GPS systems the way she was always barking out instructions. *Do this... Do that, Go here... Go there...* She reminded me of my father before I became old enough to realize I had a mind of my own. Then there was Renee who was a connoisseur of everything Southern. She loved her music slowed down and wore more platinum in her mouth than she did on her body. The first time I heard her favorite song I mistook it for some demonic devil worshiping music until I listened closely and realized it was only the lyrics to *Walk It Out.* The closest thing I found to perfection was Angela. Angela and I had a lot in common. We studied together, worked out together and broke many bed frames during our pre-mature relationship. Then little things started coming up missing; A few dollars here, a necklace there. Then one day my bank account was cleaned out. Before I could get my hands around the situation, Angela had skipped town with all of my valuables and the majority of my savings. It took a while to recover from Angela.

"Thanks for the ride Ma'," I said, jumping off the back of her bike.

"No problem baby," she said giving me a kiss and a warm smile.

"I'm going to see you tonight?"

"Of course," she smiled putting her bike in neutral and revving the engine for show.

"You meeting with the guys tonight for dominos?"

"It's Thursday, it's tradition," I reminded her.

"Really, I'm starting to think you love those dominos more than you love me."

I wasn't sure if I was more surprised about the truth in her comment, or the fact that she just threw out the "L" word. I smiled and tried to play it off.

"You still coming with me to N.Y.?"

"Of course, you know I wouldn't miss my opportunity to meet your family, Q."

With Spring Break right around the corner I purchased two round trip tickets for Nia and I back to New York for my grandparents wedding anniversary. I'd been looking forward to this trip for months since I truly hadn't been back home since I moved to Atlanta a few years ago; but first I had to make it through Music Literature class.

***

"Yes, Nick Jonas," I asked frustrated no one knew the answer.

The laughs and snickers broke out of my frustration.

"Um, my name is Tony," he responded confused.

"I know what your name is," I mumbled realizing my name memorizing trick was starting to confuse even me.

"Can none of you tell me the genre of music that came out of the 20th century?"

"Umm, Mr. Bennet, I have a question?"

"Yes, Channing Tatum," I responded on purpose to lighten the atmosphere.

"Yes Kevin," I clarified.

"It's only 2013 it won't be 2020 for another seven years."

"Thank you Kevin, but I mean 1920."

His statement caused the class to break out in laughter. He was the class clown, so I ignored his comment and tried to get the class back under control.

"Alright class, seriously. It originated within the African-American communities and requires musical instruments?"

"Mr. Bennet?"

"Yes Kendall."

"Jazz sir."

"Yes," I responded surprised. Kendall was the class model and reminded me of Jennifer Lawrence.

"Now can anyone name me a Jazz artist?

The room grew silent and I sat back in shock. Had so much of yesterday been erased that our youth only knew tomorrow? I figured someone would scream out Christian Scott or Stefon Harris, possibly a Herbie Hancock or a Wynton Marsalis but certainly a Monk or a Coltrane.

"Alicia Keys," Maurice announced knowing he had the right answer. "She plays the piano Mr. Bennet."

The class once again broke out in laughter at his comment. I wasn't taking the Columbus Short twin very serious and my class wasn't taking my questioning seriously either.

"Your partially right Maurice, but she wasn't around in the 1920's, was she?"

I glanced at the clock on the wall and was running out of time and patience.

"Homework for tonight," I announced. "I need each of you to bring the name of a true Jazz artist, one of their songs and a brief bio about them."

The moaning and eye rolling was followed by the sound of the bell. I watched as the kids rushed out of the classroom like it was a fire drill.

INSIDER TRADING

CAESAR

"Our lives are defined by opportunities, even the ones we miss." — Benjamin Button

The city known for more nightclubs than houses of worship came alive after midnight. For some, the collegiate workweek officially ended on Wednesday, leaving Thursday through Sunday up to the imagination. My short-sleeve button down exposed just enough tattoo to spark curiosity leaving the aroma of my cologne to do the rest. I traded in my usual full length zoom cushioning support for a more upscale *Cole Haan* slip-on to partake in the perks of being single. *Club Expressions* was our destination, a club known for drinks that clouded inhibitions and music that encouraged intimacy. It was the first time Marquel, Quintin, Harlem and I were catching up outside of our regular Thursday ritual.

By the time we arrived, the line outside had doubled in size. The streets were filled with expensive cars and ordinary people who spared no expense to become extraordinary once the sun set. In true celebrity fashion, we breezed past everyone straight to the front of the dormant line.

"Mr. Gibson, how's that jump shot?" the bulky bouncer supervising the line joked.

He gave a lazy impression of form and follow-through so I smiled to fuel his sarcasm.

"Still working on it," I responded giving the rest of his staff love.

"Caesar!" the annoying owner of the club shouted in amazement.

"Good to see you... so you're the reason the Fire Marshalls won't let anyone else in my club."

His phony Italian accent caused Marquel to laugh and jab me in my side with his stupidity.

"Listen, I'm putting you and your boys in your regular spot," he announced snapping at two members of his security staff to usher us in.

"You need anything you say the word... I'll make it happen."

I could barely hear the rest of his lame speech as the bass line from Mary J's new track blared from the speakers. The heat of untamed hormones and intoxicated excitement radiated from the crowded dance floor. My height and frame caused the attention of the club to shift in our direction as we followed closely behind security. We slipped past fake thugs who hugged the walls and creepy old men who circled young girls like vultures preying on the weak; past Greek steppers, wanna-be models and groupies who did anything for attention. I was a twenty-one-year old celebrity with all the extra trimmings and loving it. The two bottles waiting on ice and the plush accommodations of the V.I.P. section helped us unwind quickly.

"Remind me why we don't do this more often?" Marquel questioned causing us all to laugh.

"Seriously, what good are the perks if we never use them?" Quintin stated reaching in to break the seal on a $150,000 bottle of *Ace of Spades*.

Our attractive waitress sashayed to our booth causing our attention to shift.

"What can I do for you guys?"

Her question caused us all to look at each other and break out in laughter. She stood there with a puzzled look waiting to hear the joke.

"Yea, can I get your measurements," Quintin stated, his facial expression saying what we were all thinking.

"Can I get 10 minutes alone with you in the coat closet?" Marquel chimed in.

"Yea, mi wan meet ya muda, ya sista, ya auntie..." Harlem instructed in his deepest accent.

The waitress, finally catching on to our sarcasm impatiently awaited my response.

"Please excuse my friends, I don't believe we need anything at this time but will keep an eye out for you if we change our mind."

Everyone at the table looked at me in amazement. I could tell my comment even caught the waitress off guard as she searched the faces of my boys who were also confused.

"Way to blow the assist Caesar," Quintin stated causing us all to laugh again.

"Shut up and pass me a glass."

We all raised our glasses and toasted to friendship, a slowly dying art form.

Q is that you!

The sultriness of her voice caused us all to turn to see who required his attention.

"Nia! What are you doing here?"

He motioned for security to let her pass and she joined us at the table.

"Guys this is Nia; Nia these are my boys, Marquel, Harlem and Caesar."

"Pleasure to meet you all."

She was cute and complimented his New York style with her fashion and demeanor. The two of them sat entwined in Black love; from the look of it Q had already lost himself in her Pandora's Box.

Harlem quickly scanned the crowd and pointed out two sistas on the dance floor whose outfits lacked enough material to be considered clothing. The shadow blocking our view quickly caused confusion as my eyes worked to gain focus among the strobe lights and colorful effects.

"Sophia?" I asked surprised.

"Fancy seeing you here, I didn't think famous basketball players had time to interact with us common folk?" she announced.

The wit and style on my Caribbean bombshell, caught everyone in the booth off guard and spread a smile across my face.

"Yea mon!" I stated in my best accent causing her and her friend to laugh. "Take a seat ladies," I instructed making room for two more.

"Fella's this is my beautiful tutor Sophia; Sophia these are my peoples, Marquel, Harlem, Quintin and his girl Nia."

"Nice to meet you all, this is my girl Audry."

Harlem quickly poured them a glass and began working his magic in his deep Jamaican accent. Marquel quickly jumped in the co-pilot seat and the duo quickly became four. With the moment of solitude I sat enjoying my thoughts, the music, my freedom. My thoughts drifted to stories my mom would tell about my father in the gossip-filled salon. She assumed I was too young to understand what a personal secretary was or the meaning of a Vice President of the company. To naive to comprehend her late-night meetings and company getaways that later turned into a 6-foot basketball standout. That's when the weekly bonuses stopped, that's when my mother was surprisingly let go and when my father's white upper-class affair became too shameful. The hush money disappeared, the Range Rover in the garage vanished and the nice house in our quiet middle-class neighborhood was gone.

Just then our attractive waitress returned to our table bringing me back to reality. The entire table got quiet and watched as she sashayed over and took a seat right next to me. The boys looked at each other in shock. I quietly picked up a glass, poured her a drink and finished our night in the company of beautiful women.

Social Class

Harlem

"The only time "success" comes before "work" is in the dictionary." - unknown

The stiff wooden desk and the hum of the faded-white halogen bulbs above were clear indications the education system was purposely trying to obstruct the learning process.

I sat in class knowing I'd avoided the inevitable long enough, the time had finally come to introduce Ebony to The Empire. My plan was to continue the fabricated dance team story since experience and the rules of the game still required her distance from the truth. Just like the evolution of the game, I'd evolved from the young kid that received that package from Legacy years ago. The best thing about The Empire was our location. We were in the epicenter of teenage curiosity, the Mecca of adolescent exploration and the Motherland of youthful pleasure. College students had much more to lose; scholarships, grades and not to mention enrollment. This helped eliminate much of the common failures of empires; snitching. The next incentive was our structure. Our ability to employ numerous recruits ensured the breadcrumb trail back to us would be a long and tedious process. With all the moving parts to the business the hardest part awaited Ebony and I on the other side of the rehearsal doors.

"Look who finally decides to show up," Messiah announced noticing me enter.
"Harlem brought a Bini," Cardinal chimed in noticing Ebony trailing closely behind.
"Damn Harlem, who's the beautiful lady?" Squeeze wasted no time asking.
"Yea, and what took you so long to bring her around?"
Everyone started laughing including Ebony who was taking in all the personalities. Everyone got quiet as Allure broke the testosterone filled conversation with her presence. She circled Ebony like sharks did hopeless prey and I jumped in to save her from the awkward silence.
"Everyone I'd like you to meet Ebony, Ebony this is Cardinal... I mean Chris, we all call him Cardinal for short. Felix, a.k.a. Felony, Terrance a.k.a. Twenty/Twenty (20/20), Mike a.k.a. Messiah, Shaun a.k.a. Squeeze, Sharone a.k.a. Shaa' and the beautiful Avery a.k.a. Allure. "

"Nice to meet you all," Ebony responded overwhelmed with all the aliases.

"So Ebony, are you a cop?" Allure questioned causing the room to fill with silence.

Obviously caught off guard, Ebony turned to me for the answer.

"Chill, Ebony is our assigned Student Union Liaison for *Tropics* this year."

My response caused the tension in the air to break as everyone took a breath of relief. Allure, still weary of her intent eyed me down with a look that said, "I hope you know what you're doing."

"So this means we're going to be seeing more of this beautiful sista," Shaa responded, twirling her like ballroom dancers did their partners.

"That's right, and that means hands-off gentlemen," I responded keeping the piranhas from the fresh meat.

"So when do I get a nickname?" Ebony asked causing everyone to laugh.

"You got to earn one Ma'," Felony spoke up.

"Alright, enough clownin around we've got work to do."

Aware that play time was over everyone assumed their positions to get practice started.

"Why don't you take a seat over there," I instructed Ebony. "Practice will be short

today and we can grab something to eat after this."
She smiled and quietly made her way to the seat in the corner.

"Alright yall, let's take it from the top... 5...6, 5,6,7,8."

***

"Lil Dread, this is serious business were talking," Legacy screamed into the phone. "Dr. Bird is ready to buss una blood clot cause you're not holding up your part of the agreement."

"I'm not so lil' any more Legacy," I assured him. "You tell Dr. Bird I'm out! He can stop sending his product. I'm not selling for him anymore."

"What you mean not selling for him anymore? This was never an option, you owe him for life."

"All the money I made that man you want to tell me I owe him? I don't owe him shit."

"So that's it, you're out? You don't think there will be consequences once I tell Dr. Bird."

"I'm ready to deal with whatever consequences come along with my freedom," I screamed into the phone slamming it down on the receiver.
I was ready, ready to sever the wealth and power I created for both Dr. Bird and Legacy and start

writing my own chapter in my future. I could only hope that this decision came with a price I could afford to pay.

Black Perspective

Marquel

"It's easier to keep up than to catch up." - Bishop Lamont

Raising a half African American/half Latino son was a challenge I never thought about until he became old enough to ask the right questions. Never mind the normal difficulties of fatherhood like manners, discipline and respect; try explaining why the music we listened to was so different. Why our traditions, cultures and heritage were night and day.

> "Daddy, how come mommy's Grandma and Grandpa look so different to Nana and Pop-Pop?"

That was a question you never thought about having to explain to a three-year-old. Although his skin was brown like mine, his grandparents made sure he spoke both languages fluently, fought to make sure he had dual citizenship in both countries and made Eva promise to continue cooking their traditional meals while we were away. The constant battle between the two families made it easier for Eva and I to keep our distance and raise Darius with love and the freedom to grow with a blend of both cultures.

"What you reading Daddy?"

"This son is Cornell West."

"He has a funny beard," he laughed looking at the cover.

"I guess he does," I responded not really paying attention to that.

My son gave me the ability to look at things through a simplistic lens. Kids had the ability to make the toughest men melt, they were a sign of new life, new beginnings a chance to make right all of your wrongs.

***

There's nothing worse than 7:00 am lab on Friday morning. I'd already missed six of the ten labs this semester, so making sure I walked across the stage at graduation was going to take some serious work. At times I blamed the radio station, my wife, my son, but at the end of the day I was the only one navigating my life and I was headed full-throttle down a dead end street.

The more I listened the more I understood why I'd only attended lab twice. I was surprised at just how many people actually showed up for this class. I spotted Chaz in the corner doing his best to stay awake as the professor rambled on. Chaz and I made eye contact and he gestured for me to take the empty seat next to him. I quietly made my way through the rows like a movie go'er rushing for a refill on their large popcorn.

"Marquel, my man!" Chaz announced extending his arm for a soul clap.

His hair was now tangled and matted into dreadlocks, and the large Africa medallion around his neck proved he was still on his quest to become a soul brother.

"What's with the back-to-Africa dashiki?"

"You of all people should know Marquel, why should I conform to the stereotype of today's fashion when the "Man" is the only one profiting in the long run?"

"The Man?" I whispered, shocked by his reply.

"You know, those suits that sit in offices on the top floor and bark commands down to every-day people like you and I, the wealthy and well-off, the dictators."

Ssshhhhh... A few students hissed from behind.

"I hear you, how are things with Taye?"

"My Nubian goddess is off furthering the progression of all beautiful black women in the Mecca of social gathering."

"Oh, the hair dresser?"

"Yea man, you know she over there gossiping her ass off."

We both laughed in unison at his strange analogy.

*Ssshhhh...*We both looked back annoyed at the interruption.

"Hey we got a little situation with B.A.S.I.K."

"What kind of situation are we talking about?"

"Were getting a visit from the LAHU Board of Directors today after the show."

"What,why?"

"Your guess is as good as mine? Taye said she overheard from a few of her girls that work in the Admissions office that they feel like they're losing the authority and direction of the station. We're getting powerful Marquel and I think they want some of it."

"I thought we already went over this with them? We always had their full support when we got this station off the ground."

"Yea, but that was before we started bringing in thousands of advertising dollars, now we're a commodity."

I thought about Chaz's comments and just how powerful we'd become. Our call-in rate had skyrocketed from 30% to 80% in the last two years. Our advertising dollars tripled and we were now syndicated in seven of the nine Southern most states. The only place left for us to go was down.

***

"My father and I stood hand-in-hand during the Million Man March, I was sixteen then and since that time I've witnessed the Jena Six, the battle for the Democratic nomination between a black man and a white woman and a shocking verdict during the Trayvon Martin case." This was my moment; I stood in front of 5,000 students from around the globe at LAHU's first Activism Conference. A sea of black faces all focused on me as I spoke from the heart about my concerns for young African Americans.

"Our time is now! We can't wait for the next murder. We must take back our rights, we must take back our education and most importantly we must take back our identity!"

The tremendous roar of applause that followed my closing remarks shook the auditorium. I took my seat back on the panel of guest speakers and scanned the audience for familiar faces. I was fortunate enough to be seated next to Karen Love, the passionate and vocal activist from Chicago. The windy city had blown this chocolate goddess into Atlanta and right into the available seat next to me. Her exotic perfume filled my nostrils as I took my seat. Ms. Love greeted me with a pleasant smile as I took a sip of my cold water. Seven prominent poets, authors, radio personalities and activists cluttered the tiny stage.

Buzz... Buzz.

My *iPhone* went off on my hip.

> **Clarity:** Cute sista they sat you next to

Which meant Clarity, another of my top clients, was scattered somewhere amongst the crowd. I secretly did my best to respond without drawing too much attention.

> **Young Denzel:** I know, I'm thinking about asking her out for dinner after this is over?
> **Clarity:** I thought we were going to hang out after this?
> **Young Denzel:** What will your boyfriend have to say about that?

I put my *iPhone* on silent doing my best to block her out and listened attentively to the Q&A session. Out the corner of my eye I caught Abigail admiring me with a seductive smile. She winked at me as we briefly made eye contact. I suddenly felt like I was in the middle of a lust triangle in front of thousands of people. My wife Eva was backstage watching; Clarity and Abigail admired me from the audience and my throat suddenly felt tight with the thought of my wife suspecting something was going on. I unexpectedly felt a hand making its way up my leg. I turned my attention to Karen who was quietly sliding her hand towards my promise land.

Suddenly my Love triangle had turned into a game of four corners.

NEW YORK MINUTE

QUINTIN

"I've done so much with so little, I'm now qualified to do anything with nothing."- unknown

We stood watching the same six suitcases circle the baggage claim inside LaGuardia midday. I was getting extremely aggie because our plane landed a half hour ago and there was still no sign of our three checked bags.

> "See Q baby, this is the shit I'm talking about," Nia mumbled short of blowing her only fuse.

She was about two-seconds from going postal on the airport staff if someone didn't tell us something and quick. Jeans were replaced with tribal yoga pants that accentuated her every curve and landed carefully into her black/yellow *New Love Jordan I's*. Her *Wu-tang* baby-doll Tee cut just above her belly-button erotically displaying a well designed tattoo where her spine met her tail bone.

"New York, New York," I replied calming her down.

"There they go," she sighed seeing them slide out the tunnel.

We gathered our things and jumped in a taxi headed for my grandparents crib out in Queens.

165th Street was still buzzing. School was out so the block was filled with teens trying to be seen. My entire family was flying up for my Grandparents 50th wedding anniversary in a few days so now was the only opportunity to catch up with the streets. We caught the F-train into Manhattan, then transferred to the A, to slide by our favorite sneaker spot, *Flight Club*. We ended back up at *Pedestrian Mall* later that afternoon hoping to run into some familiar faces.

"Is that Q-Money!" a familiar voice screamed down the block.

"Profit, my dude?"

Profit was a major part of my old crew. We used to run Queens when we were young soldiers. We called ourselves *Higher Learning* cause we loved the way Ice Cube and Busta Rhymes cracked the skulls on those white supremacist in the movie. I gave him the old crew handshake surprised he still knew it. Nia noticing the commotion joined me by my side.

"Damn, and who is this Apple Bottom?" he asked taking in all her frame.

"Nia, baby this is my boy Profit, Profit this is Nia."

"Nice to meet you Ma'"

"What happened to the old crew?" I asked trying to break his trance off my lady.

"Those fools are right behind me!"

"Queens!" they all shouted.

Coming up the block I could see my old team; Showoff, a loud mouth dude from Hollis Ave. who lived up to his name by always trying to outdo me. Curfew, the youngest of the team, was from Jamaica Ave. not too far from where I stayed. We called him curfew because his parents still controlled his life and he was the only one we knew who still had to be home before the street lights came on. My Guyanese dude Logic was from Richmond Hill and the coolest of our unit because he used to have all the girls on lock. My dude Profit was my neighbor back when I lived in Rosedale and taught me everything I needed to know about the streets. Finally, Spelling...still looking like free money on a broke day; my Ex.

"What's good yall?"

"Q-Money back in the building!" Logic shouted, giving me our ceremonial dap.

"And who is this?" Spelling asked sizing Nia up with disgust.

"Spelling, this is my girl Nia."

Spelling was still untainted eye candy. Her long smooth legs stood planted elegantly in some blue

Foamposite Pro's with a mini skirt that made me want to guess what color panties she had on. Her hair was cut like Rihanna and she could pass for her twin if I hadn't known better.

"What brings you back?" Curfew asked starting to feel the heat intensifying between the two.

"My grandparents are celebrating their wedding anniversary this weekend so we'll be in town for a few days."

"You know Clean Slate is hosting a huge tournament at Marquee downtown in a few days?"

Clean Slate... the name echoed in my head like a scream in a hollow cave. Slate was my right hand and the final piece to our wrecking crew, until his jealousy over Spelling turned close friends into sworn enemies. Hate and solitude turned him into a firm believer that there was an "I" in "Team." Anything I did he naturally tried to do better and his competitive spirit was bound to end in bloodshed.

"Let's just say he's an old face I'm not interested in running into."

My comment broke the silence in the air causing everyone to laugh, but deep down that name rested on a fragile nerve.

* * *

The subway was crammed, the steel chariot gobbled up another stop of exhausted New Yorkers who commuted to the heart of the Big

Apple daily. Nia's head rested peacefully on my shoulder as we rocked to the rhythm of public transit.

"Next stop Utica," the electronic voice announced.

The train came to its normal stop and the exchange of new faces hustled on before the door closed. We watched as commuters of all shapes and sizes filled the available space in the car. Some loudmouth teenagers made their way through the crowd jumping from passenger car to passenger car. The unspoken law of subway goers was never to make eye contact so I sat analyzing traveler's footwear. Business women in high-end designer outfits exchanged 6-inch heels for the arch support of Air force ones for their lonely commute back to their boroughs. I analyzed the intricate graffiti that cluttered the tunnel walls and wondered how taggers squeezed into tight areas to permanently place their names on the walls. As I began to lose myself in thought the persistence of a passenger fighting for a proper spot, in the standing room only car, ended up directly in front of Nia and I. He rocked an exclusive pair of *SB Dunks*, some designer jeans, expensive shirt and *North Face* book bag. I sized him up trying my best not to look him directly in the face. I could feel Nia shift her weight and suddenly become uncomfortable. I turned to her to figure out her sudden change in demeanor and witnessed she was staring our anxious passenger dead in the face. I turned my attention to him as well for speechless answers. He was a fairly attractive brother with a scar similar to Nia's that made his soft exterior street approved. His scar looked like his initiation into a society that was built on a faulty foundation of drugs, sex and money. The sudden jolt of the train coming to a stop made him grab hold of the hanging handle bars as he and Nia never broke eye contact.

"Nia baby, this is our stop," I announced grabbing our bags and her hand at the same time.

We quickly exited the car and merged into the crowd of travelers emerging from the bowels of the underground dungeon.

"What was that all about?" I asked as we made our way up the steps.

"Just an old acquaintance," she responded flashing a fake smile for assurance.

Her sweaty palms and nervous demeanor suggested he was more than that.

Anniversaries are a time for reflection; a memorable day marked with gifts, smiles and the presence of loved ones. Nia and I sat shoulder to shoulder between my Uncle Lonni, and his wife Bridgette to her left and my younger cousin Rashard and his girlfriend to my right. The table was filled with family as my Grandparents continued to fill the table with delicious food. The atmosphere was like a scene out of *Soul Food* as we all crammed inside their Queens brownstone. It was very rare to catch the entire Bennet family together like this so I sat back soaking up the vibes. No one brought up my parents leaving Queens, no one mentioned my brother fighting the War, or my Dominos. I was tranquil; I was at peace, I was home.

The familiar sound of the doorbell didn't break anyone's harmony as we continued to eat and laugh. Two elderly men dressed in military uniforms filled the entrance and caused the unity that formed to cease momentarily. The look on the gentlemen's face with the most accolades said it all. I instantly turned to my mom who broke out in a shrill. Bad news had suddenly filled the room and we all realized my brother would never join us for dinner again.

PAINTING A VIVID PICTURE

CAESAR

"The artist is the voice of the people." - Alice Walker

We were immature then and always on a quest for a blank wall or an area of heavy traffic. It started with tagging, hitting up public busses in the yard to all out bombing abandoned buildings and pointless advertisements. We called ourselves the *Ruins* and made our mark by pocketing Kyrlon spray paint from our hardware store. We'd hit the streets with book bags crammed with phat caps and sketch books filled with new designs. The LAPD's tactical squads were always down our throats, so in a way the more destruction we caused, the more love we got from the streets.

I was fourteen the first time I saw the inside of a holding cell. I can still remember the smell of the aerosol cans and the mixture of paint under my fingernails as the cops placed the cold bracelets around my wrists. I was too young to understand the consequences of defacing public property but the thrill of designing my artwork on urban canvas was far greater than scribbling on pages of loose-leaf.

"How tall are you son?" the booking officer asked.

"He looks about six-foot to me," his partner chimed in dabbing my fingers in black ink.

"What's your name kid?" the same booking officer questioned filling out his paperwork.

"Caesar.... Caesar Gibson."

The two officers froze and glanced at me and Finesse in surprise.

"I knew you two looked familiar, we saw you two on that ESPN high school special the other night."

"Listen Gibson, why are you out here spray painting walls when you've got a bright future ahead of you?"

His question went in one ear and out the other as they un-cuffed us, gave us a warning and called our parents. This was the first time I witnessed the potential star power I possessed.

***

"Gentlemen, today we go into battle. Let's play smart out there, move the ball, take high percentage shots and leave everything you have on the court."

I watched as Coach paused and gathered his thoughts again. This time he spoke with much more feeling and emotions.

"We must protect our home floor, this is our house and those are your fans out there screaming for you. For the next 48 minutes I want to see all of you perform at the highest intensity level possible."

We could feel the emotion and tension coming from Coach as he shouted.

"Now everyone Crusaders on three, Crusaders on three... one...two... three CRUSADERS!" we all shouted in unison with Coach.

"Caesar, hold on for a second," Coach stopped me before I headed out the door with the rest of the team.

"How are you feeling?" he asked sounding concerned.

"Great Coach, don't worry I've been waiting for this day all my life."

"Good, good to hear that Caesar. I'm counting on you as our captain to take control of the game when these younger guys start to lose it."

"No problem Coach, I won't let you down." I said with a smile.

I walked down the long corridor that led to center court. The closer I got the louder I could hear the chant of.... CAESAR...! CAESAR...! CAESAR...! It sounded like I was the Spaniard in Gladiator that everyone couldn't wait to watch perform. The lights shined bright at the end of the hallway and the chants were becoming lighter fluid for a growing inferno. I reached the end of the tunnel and sprinted out to the center of the court to join the rest of my team. The chanting suddenly became cheers as the fans spotted me flying out of the tunnel. I stood at half court and admired my surroundings, while the rest of the team was stretching or shooting jump shots.

There was not an open seat in the entire arena; fans in the student section wore togas like citizens of a roman empire. I could read posters and signs all over the arena that read, *Hail Caesar* and other clever slogans. The press section was jammed packed as cameras and photographers lined the court with blinding flashes and lenses pointed all right at me. I waited so long for this; the spotlight, the scouts, the NBA, grades, just basketball.

    Buzzz...

The sound of the buzzer signaling the start of the game went off, our team headed over to the sideline for last minute instructions.

    "Alright fellas, let's stick to our game plan. We are going to open up with a 1-2-2 defense, alright... let's get 'em!" We broke our huddle one last time. We exchanged dap with the UCLA players at half-court and the referee gave both teams instructions.

"Here we go gentlemen! Let's play a clean game and we'll call a clean game. Does everyone understand?" Both teams nodded in unison. "Then let's get started." Big Butta gathered himself at center court for the tip off and waited for the referee to toss it up. This was it, *game time* I thought. I watched the ball hang in the air.

By halftime, we led our opponents by 10 points and my double-double was the focus of the media. Back in the locker room, Coach praised the team for the versatility of our game. When I was younger I wanted to play just like Magic and Jordan, but as I got older and developed my own game I started to finesse my game to match Chris Paul, Derek Rose and Steph Curry. I was a big guard and used it to my advantage on the court. There weren't too many point guards in college basketball that could handle the ball like I did at 6-6. My jump shot was perfect; from the flick of the wrist to my follow through on my shot. Our team went out and accomplished everything Coach expected in the opening half. We were encouraged to move the ball a bit more in the second half and stick to what worked for us in the first half, teamwork.

The second half was the complete opposite. St. John came out with a full court press and we panicked, we turned the ball over six or seven times alone in the third quarter. I could see

Coach pacing back-and-forth on the sideline as we headed into the fourth quarter only ahead by three.

This was my cue, to turn my game up as the captain, I had to take matters into my hands and pull out this victory for my team. Every possession was like conducting a symphony, we had to be on one accord to achieve a perfect sound and my job was to make sure we hit that note on every possession. I was setting up my teammates when I got double teamed, I would penetrate and dish to the open man on the wing, and scored when I had the opportunity. I glanced up at the score board and noticed that there was less than two minutes left in the game and we were barely holding on to our lead.

"Time-out, Time-out," Coach yelled from the sideline as I signaled to the ref to stop play. I guess Coach wanted to make sure we were all on the same page and eliminate any stupid mistakes in these last few minutes.

"Listen guys, hang in there... we have 60 seconds to win this game and we have the ball, so let's not rush anything. Brown, I want you to take the ball out of bounds and get it to Caesar. Caesar, I want you to run the 35 second clock down and take the last shot, is everyone clear?" he asked everyone in the huddle... and we all answered "yes."

In that moment I thought back to my meeting with Patten, the suitcase filled with money back in my dorm room and his offer. I looked around the huddle and thought, *how many of my teammates did he pitch the same offer?* The buzzer rang and we got in position for the final seconds of the game. The scoreboard read 89-91 in our favor and 60 seconds remained on the clock. Runway slapped the ball giving us the signal to run the play and I curled off the screen from Finesse, just as I was watching the ball into my hands, a UCLA player jumped the play and stole the rock. The seconds ticked as they ran back to their side of the court and set up a play. I had to turn my defense up to full notch if we were still going to win this game. I crouched down lower into my defensive stance. Their guard shook left then shook right. I was right on his every move, the seconds wound down before he faked right and went left... I was right on his hip, and then out of nowhere I was screened out by their center.

"Pick, Pick!" I shouted to let my teammates know that I lost my player in the shuffle. I watched as Smalls stepped up to pick him up, but the ball was rotated to the open forward on the wing for the three. The entire arena became silent as the ball hung in the air, I watched as it rotated over and over until.... *Swoosh!* Nothing but net. "Timeout, Timeout..." Coach yelled recognizing that there was still 25 seconds left in the game. I held my head down and walked back to the huddle. The fans in the arena were stunned as the momentum of the game had swung in the opponents' favor. Coach tried his best to regain our confidence and composure after such a big shot.

"Caesar, we're going to draw this play through you. We are only down by a point and I want you to get the ball and pound it down their throat!"

I nodded knowing what obstacle lay ahead of me; I could feel the spit in my throat start to get thick and sticky making my mouth instantly dry. I wiped my hands on my shorts to absorb the sweat that was threatening my grip on the final shot. My perspiration had already soaked my jersey and the once light nylon now added extra weight to my already weak body. I took one more look at the clock and said a quick prayer.

The inbound was perfect, I dribbled twice and made my move, I crossed over, crossed over again, put my head down and drove the lane. I could hear the crowd count the clock down, 5... 4...3... I was already at the front of the rim when I heard them yell two and threw up a floater with hands all in my face. Time literally stopped as the ball left my fingers the crowd grew silent. The ball hit the backboard, rolled around the rim... and came out.

Full Service

Marquel

"When you're older you don't take the same kind of risks you did when you were younger." – Marquel Howard

You never forget your first. You tend to reserve a special place in your heart for them. This was the relationship Abigail and I shared. She was my first client, my first friend and the first name in my client database. The truth was although she liked them tall, dark and handsome her preference was charming, cute and intellectual. Some guys kept a "black book" but my client database was digital. It kept a log of the little things, Birthday's, names of their kids, hobbies. See these little things were the difference between a one-time visit and a repeat customer. Denise was a Knicks fan and enjoyed having someone to talk trash with during the game while Carmen loved to talk and just needed someone to listen. But Abigail was there from day one, and because of that we shared a unique connection.

* * *

The annoying chime of the front door alarm jingled enough to alert us all that new money had just entered the building. The Mayor was already in the lobby gossiping with the receptionist so Zae', Denim and I jumped at the opportunity of getting the week started with our pockets filled. As I entered the lobby I noticed the familiar face of the young lady requesting assistance.

"We have openings now if you'd like," the receptionist responded.

Ms. Karen Love from the Activism Conference was back in town and looking for a little R&R from Body Language to help her unwind. We made eye contact briefly and she smiled knowing we still had unfinished business since our last encounter.

"We have four great options for you to choose from," the receptionist smiled noticing us approaching.

"The Mayor, Denim, Zae' and Young Denzel."

Ms. Love blushed as my nickname was given. She gave her four options very good consideration already knowing her selection.

"I think I'll go with Young Denzel," she responded with a serious tone.

"Right this way," I responded, leading her to my room.

As soon as I closed the door behind her, she pinned me against the door and kissed me with lustful passion.

Ms. Love was obviously unaware of how I liked to control my clients to avoid things going past second base.

"Good to see you too," I attempted to say as she pulled to get my shirt over my head.

"How did you know I worked here?"

"I know how to find what I want."

"Well what can I do for you?"

"I need a full service," she whispered locking the door and leading me to the massage table.

"Listen Karen, how was your flight?"

I asked quickly in desperation. I needed to regain control of this situation.

"Not nearly as good as this ride will be gorgeous."

"Why don't I get you a quick drink and we'll get started."

I broke her grip enough to take back the upper hand.

"All the girls in my circle talk about this place she stated making herself comfortable. Denim is that ruffneck Chris Brown type dude that dances in the kitty. Zae', is that ride at the theme park that always has a long ass line, but size isn't what impresses me."

I was making my way back with the two drinks when her last two descriptions intrigued me.

"What do they say about the Mayor?" I pushed for more.

"Some girls like those big muscular guys, you know, Mr. Marcus; bald head early 30's, model type."

"And this is what the streets are saying?"

"But Young Denzel," she whispered meeting me mid stride to make sure I understood.

"Mr. Marquel Howard himself," she took a step back in admiration.

"How do you get women to fall in love with you without sleeping with them?" I laughed at the silliness of her comment.

"We all talk about it, it's like the greatest secret," she laughed in excitement.

"Your brown is gorgeous, where did they create you?" she whispered, taking me in again.

I spun, slowly to entertain her curiosity.

"Cute..."

"Cute.!" I questioned? "Puppies are cute" I whispered walking around her realizing I could finally hear how ladies enjoyed my branding.

"Damn you know you look good boy!" she demanded, causing my nonsense filter to kick in.

"Looks? that's all women really want huh?" I walked away, causing her tone to shift.

"They say you make us laugh, your patient, charming. You're the kind of guy we can take home to our parents, you listen, you care."

She leaned in and inhaled my cologne, inhaled me like a morning yawn. I could feel that feeling in my spine like the first time Desire touched me at that party. It caused me to shift and rock my body weight like I was dizzy, I grabbed her hips for stability. She hissed taking it as an invite.

I rocked again like I had just been hit with a left and now the room started to spin.

"Something's not right," I whispered holding my head for assurance.

"No baby, it's not..." she agreed, laying me on my massage table as I struggled to keep my head up.

"Did you put something in my drink?"

"Shhh."

Dutty Fridays

Harlem

"The individual is the instrument; the mind is the senseless musician." - unknown

Tonight was a celebration, 100% of the Empire's business was finally ours. No more Legacy and no more Dr. Bird's product to burden our growth. We watched as our monthly take home skyrocketed, our membership doubled and the good times finally continued to roll.

Dutty Friday's at Club Zion was our usual spot. The tiny hole-in-the-wall club spun dancehall and culture reggae well into the a.m. hours, so I took this opportunity to initiate Ebony into our secret underground world. The Empire and I would use this spot for both business and recreation once we'd finished playing hard. I did my best to keep Ebony sheltered from the real workings of the business over the past few months since the success of *Tropics* relied on her evaluation. She would sit in on our weekly practices, launch party meetings and the entire event planning leading up to our big weekend. Everyone was growing attached to our Bajin' Liaison; and the truth was, so was I...

Zion was packed wall-to-wall with dancers and crews from all over Atlanta. The rich aroma of high grade herb mixed with the familiar scent of *Black & Milds* filled the air. There was money to be made every night, so although The Empire took a night off, our foot soldiers were making sure our revenue stream continued to flow. I spotted Ebony making her way through the entrance so I fought my way through the dance floor maze towards her. I could see the smile glide across her face and her Nubian eyes began to widen with anticipation of my approach.

"How nice of you to join us," I whispered in her ear.

"Nice bashment you got here."

That awkward moment fell upon us; that moment when chaos was happening all around but we heard nothing.

"Wsup girl!" Allure squealed noticing Ebony out the corner of her eye, her interruption only breaking our trance but not the chemistry forming between us. They both hugged and Allure pulled her off to gossip.

"You're feeling her, aren't you?" Cardinal asked, sneaking up from behind.

"It's that obvious?"

"Yea, but it's obvious she's feeling you too."

"You need to stop wasting time and take that next step."

"You know what's at stake? I have to tread lightly on this one."

"I feel you."

"Let's not worry about that now," I jabbed him changing the conversation.

Just then a new riddim came on and we all started our new moves in unison. Little did I know Ebony was watching and admiring my every move.

***

I opened the fridge in my tiny kitchen grabbing two Kola Champagnes while two beef patties in the toaster oven warmed to completion. I welcomed Ebony back to my place to unwind after the club and was mesmerized by her natural beauty that required no enhancements from *Carol's Daughters* products.

I observed as she glanced over my growing equipment and browsed through my CD collection near the stereo. She stopped on one and looked at me in amazement.

"You have the new Beres Hammond album?"

I smiled and watched her put the CD in. The smooth sounds of rockers flowed from my speakers as I joined her on my futon. I watched as she slid her foot carefully out of those brown skin-toned roman sandals making herself more comfortable.

"You like Beres?"

"Yea mon'!" she said in a cute Jamaican accent.

I watched as she took a sip of her drink and smiled at me.

"What?" she squealed noticing me staring at her.

"Nutten, I can't admire an Empress?" I asked, making her blush.

"Do you have a problem with people that drink and smoke?" I shot, taking a long gulp of my orange drink.

"What weed?" she said nonchalantly. "My brothers smoke it all the time but I've never tried it."

"Does that mean you're not willing to try? Or are you just not into that kind of stuff?"

"I've just never been offered any. I've wanted to see what the big hype was all about?"

"Would you smoke with me if I had some?"

"Sure Harlem, I feel safe with you."

I smiled and pulled my box of spinach trees from under my futon.

"Is that what it looks like," Ebony said picking up a branch and smelling it.

"It stinks!" she said throwing it back in the pile.

I went through my rolling procedure and Ebony watched on in amazement asking all sorts of questions.

"Why do you have to lick it like that?"

"How come you're throwing that stuff out?"

I just smiled and answered all her questions as best I could. When I finished I held it up to her and let her admire the re-rolled cigar.

"It's a tradition in my crib that new smokers get to light the first 'L'."

She took the blunt from me and asked a few more questions.

"Which end do I light?"

"What if I do it wrong?"

I just gave her the lighter and walked her through it. She took a big puff and let out a big cough sending smoke all over the room.

"Are you o.k.?" I asked taking the pencil-sized blunt from her and taking a drag.

She took another sip of her Cola Champagne and started giggling.

"I think I like it," she said taking the blunt back from me and hitting it the way she saw me do it.

"I love your hair Harlem," she told me playing in my locks.

My dreads had become more than just hair to me. It's who I am, my symbolism of manhood. My shoulder length mane added up like the notches in wood telling my true age.

"Thank you beautiful, that means a lot," I responded surprised by her fondness to my locks.

"Mine are taking forever to lock; will you help me grow mine?"

"Of course!" I responded excited to hear that she wanted to become everything I'd ever wanted.

***

The downtown Atlanta police station was a bit drab for being on the cleaner side of town. They always took good care of the neighborhoods around important property. It was painted in an ugly gray and white combo with reflective mirrors on all sides. The inside was a bit livelier with flat screen monitors and huge skylights on the roof, filling the lobby with warm light.

"Can I help you, sir?" the female officer asked from behind the desk noticing Faze approaching.

"Ugh.... Yea... my name is Faze. I got a call from one of your detectives asking me to meet him."

The officer picked up a thick book full of numbers and flip through. When she got to the one she was looking for, she dialed a few numbers on the phone, showing Faze one finger indicating; "Hold on a second."

When she placed the phone back on the receiver she pointed him in the direction of two sliding doors located towards the back of the building;

the sign above the doors read Investigation Department. He was instructed to find a Detective Soul who was the head of the DEA division; he would have the answers he was looking for.

Tap ... tap ... tap ...

He rapped on the door three times before being instructed to enter.
The room inside was unlike any traditional offices he'd ever seen on T.V. The room was very high-tech with monitors and computer screens all over the place. The walls were filled with cork boards littered with pinned up pictures and newspaper clippings. In the center of the mayhem sat a metallic glass desk with a huge leather chair facing backwards. The scent of an expensive cigar lingered from the opposite side of the chair and he coughed to get the smoker's attention.

"Yea, you called looking for me," a hand raised from behind the chair signaling him to stop his announcement.
"Please have a seat, sir," as the chair spun around slowly, "we know who you are Faze, or should I say Darrel Rogers?"
The detective wore a smooth brown suit the color of *Bacardi* with a matching tie and white shirt. The name plate in front of him read: Detective Soul, DEA. Mr. Soul had a polished demeanor

and the smoothness of his face made him appear like some old school gigolo.

"You are good friends with a Mr. Best, is that correct?"

"Harlem? That fake ass wanna be dealer? I wouldn't call us friends."

"We're aware of an ongoing battle between Mr. Best and your crew for turf around the LAHU campus is this correct?"

Faze was still a small time dealer but he knew that admitting anything to the DEA could implicate and complicate his growing business.

"I don't think I understand what you're asking?"

Detective Soul laughed sitting back in his leather recliner and taking another hit of his cigar.

"Mr. Rogers," he smiled back, "You can't lie to me, I'm what you kids call in the street: Five-O," he laughed again and spun around punching some buttons on his computer behind him. He flipped his flat screen monitor around on his desk to face Faze and proceeded.

"What we have here is a case that has been on-going for quite some time. There has been a rash of arrest on the Westside of Atlanta with heavy busts of narcotics and pills. We have witnesses identifying you as a person of interest."

He continued pressing more buttons on his keyboard.

"We are aware of both your operations and their movements."

He sat back in his chair amazed.

"What do you want from me?"

"I thought you'd never ask," Detective Soul continued. "We are coming to you Faze because you will be our eyes and ears on the streets. Mr. Best and his operations are raking in half-a-million dollars a week. Right now he has a team of people running the show and we have not been able to identify or pin anything on them the past three years. Their operation is so widespread and exchanges so many hands that we have yet to build a solid case on any of them."

"You're kidding me? That fake rasta and his crew are making that much money? We robbed one of his runners a few months back and came off with some heavy weight, but I never thought they could do that much damage."

"Well Faze, we have reason to believe that his roots are deeper than they may appear. Right now we have agents who suppose he has Narcotics and pills coming in from the Caribbean, Mexico and the West Coast. He has major operations in California, New York and Miami making more money than you could ever imagine."

Faze sat back in amazement. The few thousand dollars and handful of weight he knocked off from his runner were nothing but gas money. The more he thought about it the more he became pissed off and furious that Harlem and his crew were the reason his money was coming up short all these years.

"What do you need to know?"

PEACE OF MIND

QUINTIN

"Be ashamed to die until you have done something great for humanity." – unknown

The age of the digital DJ was upon us. Crates of records were consolidated onto laptop hard drives and hand-held *iPods* that could out play any Disc Jockey with the right amount of bandwidth. It was a sin how this generation was deprived the etched grooves of vinyl records, the simultaneous pressing of play and record on TDK tapes and the slow extinction of Compact Discs.

Quincy, Spelling and I sat huddled in the corner of the subway car on the way to Manhattan. Word was, Clean Slate was welcoming all contenders to a Dominos championship and the opportunity to dethrone the champ was in my sites. When word that the Grandson of the legendary Bennet family had taken up the family tradition, the entire borough was expected to turnout for the show. Quincy sat making jokes to lighten the mood while Spelling and I laughed at his immature humor. My domino's sat cradled in a *North Face* book bag as I quietly sat replaying moves in my head. Noticing my nervous demeanor Spelling rubbed my shoulder to sooth the tension. The more I thought back to that night the more the face of that guy on the subway started to reappear; the scar, the expression. That joker was a part of Slates crew. I remember seeing that same scar on the face of his new hit man that night at the competition. That was the night I beat Clean Slate, the same night Spelling became pregnant and the last time the three of us hung out together.

***

They explained the cause of death was a roadside I.E.D. So many lives had been lost to this cowardly form of War and now my baby brother had become a casualty. The stock market was at an all time low and a gallon of gas cost more than a gallon of milk.

I had to hit the streets of NY for answers. My family was hysterical, Nia wouldn't stop crying and I was beginning to feel boxed in by the overwhelming flood of emotions. The last memory of my brother was his eighteenth birthday. He was being deployed on his first tour so we all braced for the worst and hoped for the best. My father and I argued all weekend about me choosing Education as my major at LAHU. The more we argued the more assured I felt in my decision. The only problem was I chose to pursue music as my future; the armed forces choose my brother to fight for his.

I rode the trains for hours. It was the first time the stiff plastic seats had no feeling, the noisy subway cars held no sound and the tunnels I traveled through shared the same sentiments I felt hollow and empty. The tracks ended at the Queens Center stop and I emerged from my underground sorrow. I needed to be around familiar faces so I flagged down a dollar taxi over to Profits crib.

    "Q, what's good? Yo, is everything iight kid? You look terrible."

    "It's my brother, he got knocked."

    "Damn, come in."

Curfew and Logic were already in his living room screaming at the PS3 console on his flat screen.

    "What's good fellas?"

    "What's good Queens," they responded screaming at the television.

Profit had already made his way back to the room with a few glasses and a bottle of Hennessey.

    "Tell me what happened?" Profit asked pouring my glass halfway and doing the same with his.

I quickly swallowed the contents and gathered my thoughts. Curfew and Logic noticing my condition stopped playing and joined us.

    "They sent soldiers by the spot today. We were all loungin' enjoying the positive vibes and then there was a knock on the door. Say's his unit was coming back from a seven-day mission and the truck he was traveling in was hit by a road-side I.E.D. killing them all."

"Damn kid," Logic stated holding his head down.

I could hear Profit pouring more of the brown liquid in my glass.

"I was saving this for later, but I think we could use this," Curfew chimed in pulling out a spliff the size of a glue stick.

"I told Quincy that armed forces move was a death trap, but he wouldn't listen."

"Listen, we all have a chosen path we must walk and Quincy knew what he was getting into and the consequences involved," Logic spoke up.

"Word!" everyone mumbled in unison.

I threw back another shot and took a toke or two of the spliff that was making its way around the room. We all talked and reminisced about life, family and our past for hours. The combination of the smoked filled room and the bottom of the bottle numbed the pain of my loss. It was getting late and I needed to get back home before the Bennet family began to worry about their only remaining son.

Hours later I was knocking on the window of Spelling's apartment. I was led there by memory and intoxication; a deadly combination when grieving.

"Queens, is that you? Get in here, what the hell are you doing?"

"You smell like a wino, do you have any idea what time it is?"

"You were always my best friend Spell," I slurred trying to stand up straight.

The soft glow of her television in the background was the only light that illuminated her room.

"It's Quincy,"

"What about him, is he back home?"

"He's dead!"

At that moment the room fell silent. Quincy had played just as an important role in her life too. She hugged me sensing the hurt and loss I was feeling. I sunk my head into her soft skin and inhaled her essence. Everything was as I remembered it; the off-white paint on her walls, the twin size bed against the corner wall and her wooden desk near the window. It had been years since I'd step foot in her house but the memory was like yesterday.

"I'm so sorry Queens," she cried on my shoulder.

I softly kissed her neck and embraced her the way old lovers did when they were trying to re-familiarize themselves with well charted areas.

In that moment we kissed.

School Of Hard Knocks

Caesar

"A man's true worth is not measured by what he stands to gain, but rather what he stands to lose." - unknown

Losing was an unfamiliar feeling, so I handled it the only way I knew how; in the arms of a new woman. I called Celeste, my half-Caucasian/half-Spanish Musiq Soulchild *Buddy*, whose complexion matched mine. I asked her to meet me at my lavish on-campus student accommodations later that night and like clockwork there was a knock at my door. I was greeted by her low-cut wife beater that hugged her upper body just right. The tiny white cloth stopped right above her waistline exposing the diamond that hung from the center of her belly button. The low rider jeans squeezed her hips and drew attention to her already tiny waist. Celeste was only 5-8" but her heels made her an even 6-0" and tall enough for her to reach the center of my chest. I let her in and the scent of her perfume tickled my senses like airborne Viagra. The tattoo on her lower back screamed like a fast-food sign: *Have it your way.* She took a seat on the bed crossing her legs and taking in the sites and surroundings of my dorm room.

"I like your place," she stated picking up a pair of custom *Lebron IX's* that had just arrived in the mail.

"Thanks!" I replied as I headed to the bathroom to freshen up.

"Make yourself at home."

"So you weren't kidding about having a lot of sneakers?"

"You thought I was?"

I could hear her making her way around the room amazed by everything.

"I really like your drawings, how long have you been drawing?"

"Since I was old enough to hold a crayon."

"That long, huh?"

Her statement was followed by some papers shuffling on my desk. I paid her no mind as I played out tonight's escapades in my mind. I took one last look in the mirror and headed back out to prove the hype behind the name was real. I was startled when I came out to see Celeste thumbing through a stack of hundreds like an Aquanza Cadogan novel.

"There's got to be at least a half a million dollars here?" She stated looking back at me in amazement

"Yea," I admitted taking a seat next to her.

"What are you doing? Let's go spend some of this."

"Spending it could jeopardize my draft eligibility at the end of the year," I admitted picking up a stack of hundreds as well.

"Yea, but you won't jeopardize anything if nobody knows?"

Celeste had a point. Till now, no one was aware that I had accumulated this wealth except Celeste and Patten himself. I watched as Celeste picked up two more handfuls of money and laughed in amazement. We made eye contact for a minute and broke out in laughter together. Celeste threw her handful of money at me sending bills flying all over the room. Shocked, I threw my handful back at her causing more money to scatter around the room. Celeste squirmed and giggled as we rolled and kissed on the bed littered in big face bills, her smell arousing me, the money fueling me.

***

The LAHU track stadium was filled to capacity. The media frenzy was in town to highlight someone other than me for a change. The talented Tia Springs was in town and the track enthusiasts were all vying to get a glimpse of the countries newest sensation; everyone including myself.

All shades of brown filled the field from various schools around the Southeast. They were all built like thoroughbreds; calves and legs twice the size of Natasha Hastings and all squeezed into tiny shorts that were pleased to accommodate. I laughed as I watched every one do their best to hide from the sun under umbrellas and sun hats. I guess that was the difference between black and white people; *we were always trying to hide from the sun while they were trying to bathe in it*. I was so into crowd gazing that I didn't notice the amount of attention being placed on me. I noticed people from the stands starting to recognize me and I could hear the whispers:

"Isn't that Caesar Gibson?"

"Hey look its Caesar!"

A few groupies wasted no time surrounding me with giggles and requests for autographs, I signed as many as I could, but my mind set was to get a glimpse of Ms. Springs. I spotted her team from Miami out in the corner of the field stretching and tried to fight my way out of the mob that was starting to form.

"Hey! Make room, make room," my boy Tiny shouted backing the crowd up with his deep voice. Tiny was head of campus security and earned the name from his Silverback Gorilla frame. I'd gotten to know all of campus security pretty well, since my popularity ensured that I could no longer travel without escorted security.

"Tiny to the rescue again," I joked.

"What you doing out here superstar?" he asked throwing a fake jab to my shoulder.

"You know you can't just show up at events like this without letting us know first."

"I know, I know. I heard the notorious Tia Springs was going to be here, I had to see for myself."

"She's the reason why everyone else is out here," he joked.

"Why you trying to get at the young sista'?" he asked trying to lead me through the sea of fans.

We made it to his golf cart near the end of the track and jumped inside leaving everyone in a trail of dust.

"I'm going to take you where you can watch the race with a little more privacy," he said swerving in and out of cones and hurdles.

Tiny pulled up to a tent near the center of the field that was nicely shaded and surrounded with water coolers.

"This is where they have security staying, you should be safe here," he said.

I got out the cart and took a seat near the mist fan that kept a steady stream of cool air blowing.

Just then Tiny's radio went off, "We have a disturbance near the restrooms, we need security there immediately," a female voice announced from his walkie-talkie.

"I'll be back in a few," Tiny said jumping back in his cart.

"Handle that, toy cop," I yelled and he shot me the bird driving back off in the hot sun. I sat back and soaked up the scene, my attention was quickly drawn to Tia as she stretched with another partner in the sun. I was amazed by her flexibility, I watched her lean over and place her head to the floor.

"Up next, the Ladies 100 meters," the announcer yelled over the intercom. Tia stripped out of her warm ups and took one last stretch, we made eye contact for a second and a smile lit up across her face. She was perfect, everything about her was just flawless. I watched as she took her spot in the blocks and shook those thick thighs one last time before getting down into her starting position.

"Runners on your mark....!" Everyone got down real low in their blocks, heads down and focused.

"Get set...!" They all rose and put all the pressure on the tips of their fingers. I could feel the tension in the air and I got up out of my seat to get a better look.

"Bang...!" the crack of the gun caused the crowd to rise and scream in excitement.

Tia immediately jumped out from the rest of the pack. The power and grace in her stride made her stand out like Usain Bolt. The muscles in her legs carried her like a queen in a chariot being led by white stallions. She flashed through the finish line in a blur and the crowd got silent waiting to see her time flash on the screen. 11.25 popped up on the screen and the fans went insane, as her time was shy of a world record by a second and some change. I was impressed, she was good and I admired that. I observed as she celebrated with her team and then quickly surrounded by the media and paparazzi shooting photos and asking questions. Tiny came back with his cart and wheeled me back out of there while the crowd and the media were still distracted with their celebration.

"How'd you like that?" Tiny asked, "How'd you like that?

All I could say was, "She's fast... she is fast."

***

The media can be your best friend and your worst enemy all at the same time. I thumbed through the channels stopping on ESPN, who had a picture of my face on the screen; I turned up the volume to hear what Stuart Scott was saying.

"To add more heat to the fire brewing down in Georgia, the Crusaders star point guard, Caesar Gibson, after alleged rumors of talking to sports agents now has bigger problems on his hands. Mr. Gibson was recently spotted with Celeste Johnson, a noted and famous adult entertainer in the Atlanta area. I wonder if that had anything to do with the loss down there," Scott reported trying to ruin my reputation.

Adult Entertainer, I thought.

"Damn, just what I needed."

Immediately my dorm room phone started to ring.

"Hello," I asked wondering who could have such bad timing.

"Caesar, are you watching the television?" my mother shouted into the telephone.

"Yea, I'm watching it."

"What is all this Adult Entertainer stuff they talking about honey?"

"Are you hoe'ing out there on campus?"

"No mom, I had no idea she was a porn star."

"Well, you have to be careful about who you associate yourself with, this kind of stuff is not good publicity, plus I know I didn't raise no hoe." She said filling in her last two cents just as the phone beeped signaling another call.

"Mom I have to go, someone else is on the other line."

"Alright baby give me a call later, ok?" I rushed her off the phone and answered the next call.

"Hello?"

"Yea Caesar, this is Coach. Is this true

what I'm watching on TV."

Damn, I thought to myself news sure does travel fast.

"What the hell were you doing this weekend?" Coach asked.

"Coach I'll have to tell you about it later," I responded not having enough time to digest what was really going down.

Before I could get out my next sentence, another call interrupted our conversation.

"Coach, I'm going to have to call you back, I have another call."

"Hello?"

"Good evening Mr. Gibson. This is Mr. Patten's secretary, I have a message for you," I listened as she began.

"Mr. Patten would like to meet with you," she said followed by a dial tone.

After they aired my dirty laundry all over ESPN, all the other news channels began their coverage on me and the Crusaders:

"Does Caesar Gibson have the potential to take this team to another final four?"

"I don't know what those kids would do down there in Atlanta without Gibson?"

Day-in and day-out the televisions networks replayed comments like these and it wasn't long before these comments affect the chemistry of our squad. Simple was hard enough; juggling my classes, passing my exams and now this.

Declaring A Major

Marquel

"80% of the final exam will be based on the one lecture you missed and the one book you didn't read..." - unknown

I woke up to the soft sounds of Cody ChesnuTT crooning softly in the background as Ms. Love slow danced on my lap. I could feel the warmth of her insides on my pelvis and the intense sensation meant she didn't bother putting protection on me. I struggled in a panic and could feel the bondage of my hands just around the wrist.

"What's my name?" Karen whispered as she noticed me coming around.

Too drugged to formulate words she asked again, this time louder and more aggressive.

"What's my name Marquel?"

This time I could feel the heat of an open palm across my face.

Did this chick just slap me?

Whack... Whack...

Two more openhanded swats at my face as I instantly became sane.

> "What the hell is wrong with you Karen!" I shouted doing my best to get up and push her off. The restraints on my wrists keeping me in place like white tourist kept their kids on vacation.
> "Untie me right now Karen!"
> "Why Young Denzel? You don't like to be hit?"

Slap... Slap...

Those two slaps becoming one too many, I pulled feverously at the professional sailor knots bonding my arms. Karen, still bouncing up and down on my lap began to laugh and fling her hair like she was possessed by the idiot Gods.

> "I get to be the one that slept with the un-sleepable," she laughed.

At this point Karen had lost all common sense but my second head however, remained harder than a red wood pencil during a pencil fight causing Karen to continue her rant.

> "This is no longer funny Ms. Love, if you don't untie me right now there's going to be some serious problems."
> "Shut up!"

Whack... Whack...

"I heard you were married."

"Karen I don't care what you heard, I need you to stop." I said in a calm and rational voice.

"I want you to get off me, untie my hands and we'll act like this little incident never happened."

The more I talked the more she continued to rock her hips searching for her climax. Under normal circumstances I would have invited this type of domination, but six slaps later I wanted out and as far away as possible from her lunacy.

"You like that daddy?" she asked picking up her tempo. "Does your wife do you like this?

I refused to answer just wanting her to hurry up and get it over with. Then reality settled in; this was flat out rape. The word "stop" only fueled her wildfire and turned my pleasure into anger; my anger into hate and my hate into violation. Karen arched her back, I could feel her pelvic muscles contracting as she dug her nails into my chest. She screamed slightly exploding like she had lost control of her bladder soaking the already sweaty table. She kissed me in exhaustion and slapped me one more time as she recovered from her energy draining exercise.

"Looks like your streak of not sleeping with women is over Marquel."

I watched as she quickly got dressed and walked out the room leaving me laying there naked, soaked and bonded.

* * *

I glanced around the room for something to keep my mind off Karen Love. I knew Eva could tell something was wrong because I wasn't myself, I felt violated, used. I spent more time at the station because I couldn't look her in the face anymore.

I cringed as I watched nasty Sunny chewing his nails in the corner. Nasty Sunny was the type of guy that never washed his hands after he used the bathroom and wasn't ashamed of it. To the right of me was motor-mouth Gigi who always had a damn Bluetooth in her ear. It took the entire school year for me to realize she wasn't talking to herself, it was that tiny ear piece hidden under her hair that gave away her secret. The class moaned in unison as Devon, the professor's pet, stood with another wrong answer. He was the kind of person with big dreams but little plans. We all broke out in laughter as a wad of paper hit him in the back of the head. I pulled out my *iPhone* to check my messages. This was the third day I'd blown off Desire and Body Language so I was sure her or The Mayor would feel a certain way about their money coming up short.

Abigail: Hey Marquel, how you been?

YoungDenzel: Hey you, I've been better.

Abigail: I missed you yesterday, I thought we were going to hang?

YoungDenzel: Sorry, I've been under the weather.

Just as I was running out of excuses to give Abigail a second *iMessage* interrupted our conversation.

Chaz: Yo Marquel, there's some crazy video that's gone viral on you.

YoungDenzel: What are you talking about?

Chaz: Taye just called me and told me her and her girls have been watching a link that's been floating around the net, and you're on it.

What video...? I thought.

YoungDenzel: Thanks for the heads up man.

I quickly pulled up my *Facebook* page and as Chaz stated the very first link posted on my wall took you straight to a *YouTube* video. The first few minutes of the video showed Karen Love ranting and raving about nothing. I put my earphones in my ear to listen closely to her speech. The video then cut to us the night she went crazy. It showed me laid out bonded to my massage table being slapped and manhandled. I sat up in my seat thinking, *she was taping this?*

I instantly went from confusion to concern. If Taye and her girls had already seen this how many other people may have seen it? As I searched for answers, gossip Gigi turned and looked at me with a smile. A smile that said the word had already spread. A few seconds later phones began to vibrate all around the room with urgent messages. I hid my face in embarrassment as the professor wrapped up his lecture and dismissed the class for the afternoon. As the class made a mad dash for the door I sat in my desk ashamed to face the music.

TWELVE CREDITS

HARLEM

"Thought + Imagination = Creativity; Preparation + Opportunity = Chance." - Harlem Best

The key to promotions was timing. We needed to touch as many people as possible so we all met mid-day in the campus union. Shaa' nonchalantly pulled out his mini sound system and cued up the track. The melodic sounds of Benjai; *The People's Champion* slowly caused attention to shift in our direction. We'd rehearsed three-days a week for months and now it was time to go out and have some fun. I joined Allure in the middle of the Union as Shaa' began recording our hips rocking in unison. We paused for a moment to make sure we had everyone's attention and then the rest of the Empire started to follow the steps in unison. By mid song we had everyone rocking and swaying to the island vibe. The roar of applause in the student union was the sign of approval we needed to know we were ready for

Tropics. I watched as the team handed out fliers for the big event and smiled as I noticed Ebony in the crowd.

"You guys are amazing!" she yelled jumping into my arms.

"I'm glad you liked."

"Are you kidding? Me and every other girl out here," she kissed me sounding slightly jealous.

"Well there is only one girl out here I'm trying to impress."

We both turned our attention to Shaa' who was punching away at his *iPad* next to us.

"How does it look?" I asked noticing his focus.

"Amazing, we're already viral on *YouTube*."

"Respect!"

Things were finally coming together and Ebony and I were getting closer by the minute.

***

The distinct lobby of Regency Dispensary was undersized and eerily quiet. The odd furniture matched the confusing pictures hanging from the walls and the abundance of stainless steel portrayed a scientific and sterile atmosphere. I was here to pick up my information for the growing convention so my adrenaline was pumping with excitement. I tied my locks back and approached the receptionist with a smile.

"I'm here to pick up my booth assignment for the growing convention."

I could smell her fear like an expensive perfume from behind the desk. If this were a bank, she would have already reached for the silent alarm under the counter to alert the authorities.

"And you are?"

"Best, Harlem Best."

I watched as she punched a few keys on her keyboard while keeping a watchful eye on me.

"Can I see some form of identification?"

Her question instantly gave me the impression that I was being picked from a police line-up. The wads of cash in my pockets, expensive name-brand glasses on my face and hundred dollar suit meant nothing; to her I was just another black kid looking for a hand out.

"Is there a problem?" I asked already knowing the answer.

"Sorry Mr. Best, you just can't be too careful nowadays," she replied pulling a large envelope from her cabinet and handing it to me.

"This packet contains all the information you will need for the convention. Your booth number will be 25 and we ask that all participating growers meet with our panel one week prior to the convention to review all new strains."

"How many growers are in this year's convention?"

"Right now only 25 have been given an invitation."

"So that means that I have the last booth? Can you show me where that's located on the map?"

"How and when will I know when I need to meet with the panel to review my strains?"

"We'll give you a call."

Yea right, I thought.

Little did this secretary know that her statement was a re-occurring statement that hardly came to fruition. I picked up my packet and headed straight for the exit. I could feel the eyes of everyone in the room follow me until the electric doors closed behind me.

I immediately called my little brother Arius to check up on him. This was his Senior year in high school and he thought his big brothers hustle was his ticket to fame. I wanted him to stay far away from drugs and the corruption that came along with it. I made sure he had his nice sneakers and cool electronics but I never wanted him to get his hands on any product, I didn't want him distributing and I certainly didn't want him to get a taste of the money that came along with the business.

"Arius, wha gwan?"

"Big Bro, nothing."

"How's Granny and Grandfather?"

"Granny stay in the kitchen and Grandfather said he's running low on his medicine."

"Jesus, that man burns like a chimney."

"Always has, when you going to let me help you make some money."

"You know that's not going to happen."

"Come on, I've got a following of high school kids ready to line up and buy big!"

"I'm not hearing you."

"Come on Prom is right around the corner, I'll give you ten percent."

"Ten percent! I'm the one fronting the product, bruh."

"I'll just go ask Legacy or better yet, Dr. Bird."

"Arius, I don't ever want you talking to them you hear me!"

"I know, I know."

"Just go to school and learn, don't be in such a hurry to grow up."

I could tell by his silence he was pissed but that's what big brothers did – protect their family.

Diversifying My Portfolio

Caesar

"The real measure of your wealth is how much you'd be worth if you lost all your money." - unknown

As our bus pulled up in front of the hotel in Durham, NC I turned off my *iPod* and pulled my seat back into its up-right position. I quickly gathered up my stuff and headed for the front of the bus. I could see an ocean of people filling the sidewalk between the hotel entrance and the bus. I stepped off the bus to a chorus of cheers and screams, photographers shooting photos and fans yelling for autographs. I was being pulled in all directions until security formed a wall around me and escorted me safely into the lobby.

We still had to meet for a team dinner in twenty minutes and then off to the arena for shoot around. I grabbed my bags and headed to the elevators exhausted. My large frame filled most of the tiny elevator and I immediately noticed a cute sista' holding down her corner. I pushed six on the console and dropped my bag to the floor.

"That's strange, I'm getting off on that floor too," her soft voice explained, flashing her perfect smile.

"Really? What brings you to North Carolina?" I probed trying to get more answers.

"Well, I'm a student at UNC. I work here on the weekends for my internship."

"Well, It's a pleasure to meet you and I'm sorry we didn't meet sooner," I replied making her smile again.

"Well my girls and I are having a party tonight. We would love it if you and some of your friends could stop by?"

The elevator came to a slow stop on the sixth floor, the ding of the bell notifying us of our arrival.

"I don't know, we'll see." I responded as she got off the elevator and headed left down the hallway.

I watched as she sashayed down the hall and thought *damn*, as I pushed my key into the door.

***

My team gathered at half court in celebration as the score board read: Crusaders 84 - Tar Heels 72. This victory put us one game away from a fourth divisional title and an automatic bid to the NCAA tournament. We all ran back to our locker room in excitement to share this enjoyment with our coaching staff. Before I could get to the tunnel with the rest of my team, I was stopped by an anxious reporter.

"Excuse me Mr. Gibson... Mr. Gibson, how does it feel to lead your team to another win after that heartbreaking opener a few months ago?"

"Well it was a team effort. We all did a tremendous job of distributing the basketball and making big shots when it counted."

"Well that's a modest answer," she responded back into the camera, "Considering you scored 32 points, 12 assists and 7 boards, not to mention the twelve game winning streak of the Crusaders."

"Tonight my team just wanted it more, like I said everyone contributed to our victory tonight."

"Well, what can we expect from the Crusaders the rest of the season considering the rumors circulating around your recent incidents?"

"I can assure everyone out there that no rumors can stop this team from achieving the championship again this year."

****

It was almost midnight when we rang the doorbell to the apartment. I brought Smalls, Runway and Finesse with me because we were all seniors and less likely to face punishment since this was our final semester. It was always intimidating to walk into a house party with a crew full of six footers but that's just how life was for us; all eyes were on us. I rang the bell twice and waited for an answer, we could hear the DJ inside scratching some new *T.I.* single. You could almost feel the energy of the party from the other side of the door. The beautiful intern greeted us at the door and I could tell by her reaction that she was already drunk.

> "Caesar," she screamed jumping into my arms.

This was definitely not the same sophisticated intern I'd run into on the elevator. Her outfit was a lot shorter and much more revealing. I could smell the liquor on her breath as she kissed me on my cheek and looked over my entourage.

> "And who are these fine brothas you brought along?" she asked looking everyone over. "Well don't just stand there come in, come in."

Her apartment was big; the vaulted ceilings accommodated our six-foot-frames easily and the apartment was packed from corner to corner with people. The DJ was set up near the window and his tiny light was the only illumination that filled the space. We fought our way through the crowd of people dancing, making out or intoxicated and made our way to the bar set up in the kitchen.

"I was hoping you had something a bit stronger?" I asked feeling the need to join the rest of the party in drunken celebration.

"Now you're talking my language," she whispered in my ear and winked.

The music pumpin' inside her apartment made the bones in your body vibrate. Despite having to sign a few autographs for a few fans, the handful of young ladies wearing pink and green drew the attention of the guys. We each paired up with one and did our best to communicate over the loud music. Smalls and Runway, took their new friends upstairs after a few minutes of convo and Finesse took his to the balcony. I stood there whispering some fly shit into the ear of my hotel intern.

"I like your style, what's your name?"

"Asia."

"What you studying?"

"Accounting."

"So you can help me count all this money when I make it to the big league?"

The heat and noise eventually drew us out front for fresh air and better perspective. I don't know if it was the liquor or the atmosphere but the more we talked the more it seemed like Asia had a good head on her shoulders. It didn't affect her that I was Caesar Gibson, or that I was one of the most highly sought after seniors in this year's draft.

"So what time are you kicking everyone out?" I asked trying to make my last night in town a more memorable one.

"I was thinking about pulling the plug any minute now."

Before I could respond to her comment, a *Denali* pulled up on the sidewalk with the headlights blaring right on us. Three big brothers jumped out and stood over us as we sat on the front porch.

"What are you doing with my lady?" the last one out the car shouted.

His height and tattoos similar to the players from the team we beat earlier tonight.

"Is there a problem here?" Finesse shouted.

"Yea if you Atlanta boys think you can just come up here and do whatever you want, you got another thing coming!" He yelled lunging at us.

By the time I could react it was an all out brawl and everyone was in a fight of their own. Red and blue lights followed by sirens broke the panic and commotion in the front yard. The crowd scattered at the site of law officials and the police stood there with their guns drawn.

"Everybody freeze!" they shouted directing all of us to lay face down on the ground.

TROPICS

HARLEM

"Every day the bucket a-go a well, one day the bottom a-go drop out." - Bob Marley

The sounds of Movado echoed throughout my apartment as I celebrated another harvest of product successfully distributed just in time for *Tropics* weekend. Thursday night Ebony would lead our Carib Conference that touched on gun violence, safe sex and other issues concerning Caribbean youth. Friday the Empire would host a soccer tournament and Island Splash social in preparation for the huge *Tropics* pre-party on Saturday. Some of the biggest dancehall crews had pre-registered for the competition and the weekend attendance had exceeded our expectations. Mad Hype, RDX and Timeless Crew were just some of the dance teams that had already arrived in town so we'd meet tonight one last time to finalize everything.

The riddim needed a sound clash; the sound clash needed a selector and the selector needed dancers to move the crowd, a simple supply and demand that created another need for the Empire. In the final round only three teams remained: Timeless Crew, Black Bringers and The Empire. The final dance off would give the three remaining teams an opportunity to show the crowd all they had leaving them to decide the winners of this year's *Tropics*. Timeless Crew blew everyone away with a new riddim that had everyone swaying to the melodic beat. I caught myself tapping my foot as they filled the stage with synchronized arm and waist movements that harmonized with every change in the beat. The crowd let out a tremendous roar of applause as I turned to witness nervousness fill the faces of the members of the Empire.

"Up next, Black Bringers Crew!" the selector screamed into the microphone.

I was already concerned about BBC because they've been known to use their looks to persuade the crowd. Their set opened with a slow riddim causing a few lighters to flicker around the room. The selector then pulled up the riddim and the next thing I could remember was half naked bodies dutty whining in the center of the stage. All the women started screaming as they gyrated and flexed every possible muscle in their body. I found myself having to contain Allure who was now fanning herself after her sudden rise in blood pressure. Bullhorns started going off simultaneously around the room as the entire building awaited the next one hundred and eighty seconds; the months of preparation, the hours of practice and the expectation from the audience caused the anticipation in the room to mount. I nodded at Cardinal and then Allure, making sure their eyes were filled with the same confidence as mine. The lights dimmed, the selector cued the riddim and the smile that spread across Ebony's face were the last things I could remember before we set it off.

* * *

The cookout was in full swing by the time we got to my grandparents house. The smell of Jerk Chicken on the grill filled the warm Atlanta air as Ebony and I entered walking hand in hand. I was proud because we had solidified yet another *Tropics* trophy and the Empire would go down in LAHU history. Some Beenie Man was blaring out of the sound system and the backyard was already packed.

"Yo mon!" Squeeze joked smelling like he'd already swallowed the entire bottle of Belvedere. "We killed them dudes yesterday," he mumbled taking a bite out of his Beef Patty.

Messiah and Shaa' popped up along with Felony and Allure. It felt good to be surrounded by family and today was the day that I decided to have Ebony meet mine.

Already aware that we needed to discuss business, Allure led Ebony off into the corner to gossip.

"I got the 411 on that snitch Faze," 20/20 whispered.

"Word on the streets is that Faze is running his mouth to the DEA," Cardinal announced.

"So where do we go from here?"

"I say we run up on these clowns and show them who's who," 20/20 spoke up.

"Retaliation will only bring more heat to an already boiling situation," I spoke up. "Plus if he's working with the cops the last thing we need is a dead informant."

The two of them stood there worried knowing that Faze and his crew had become that Trojan horse we'd just let through our gates and the fall of our Empire was inevitable.

"Excuse me ya'll, I'm going to find my Grandparents."

I headed off into the crowd to find Ebony; the time had finally come to introduce her to my family. I opened the door to the house and was immediately greeted by the scent of the islands in the kitchen. My grandfather was jammin' some Gregory Isaacs out of his old stereo and the atmosphere instantly made me miss my mother.

"Harlem! Whata gwan boy?"

"Nuttin' a gwan, granny, I bring somebody fi ya meet."

"Oh, I wish you'd da tell mi you was bringin' company, I wudda put on something proppa."

"Don't worry, bout' it... Granny dis Ebony, Ebony dis is mi grandmother."

I watched as they exchanged hugs and greetings of excitement. I left the two in search of my grandfather who was most likely in his den. He was usually sitting in his rocker blazin' what he considered medicine.

"Wha gwan?" he asked putting out his spliff and giving me a hug.

"All fruits ripe Grandfather, I bring somebody fi' ya' meet."

"Who? A gal?"

"Zeen"

I followed him as we both headed to the kitchen. Old age and years of smoking had made him slow and feeble so I braced him for support.

"Ahh, Ebony dis is mi husban'," granny explained already introducing the two before I could do the honors.

"Pleasure fi meet you, Ebony," my grandfather said shaking her hand.

"You introduce her to ya brotha yet?"

"No Grandfather, where is he?"

"Mussy back a yaad playing dem video games or something."

"Arius!" they both shouted as if common place around the house.

"Yes Granny!" he shouted peeking around the corner?

"Wsup, big bro?"

"Everything is everything."

"I want you to meet someone, this is Ebony."

"Pleasure to meet you," he said, looking her over.

"You got a sister that looks as good as you?"

"Boy look here!" my grandmother shouted.

"Your eyes pass that girl."

We all laughed at his comment, his humor a queue for us to all join the rest of our guest outside.

As afternoon fell on our celebration, I pulled Ebony aside to show her one of my many secrets. She followed me out the house towards my grandfather's old shed.

"Where are we going Harlem?" she asked curious about what was so special in the back of the house.

I opened the door to the shed that was filled with dust, cobwebs and my grandfather's old '76 Cutlass that stopped working years ago. I took her by the hand and led her to the back of the shed to a pile of boxes that were stacked about waist high. I moved a few to the side to display a tiny trap door hidden under the false storage. Ebony leaned in close to me as I blew the dust off the cover and pulled opened the door. She turned and looked at me as she witnessed the metal door with only a handle and a spinning combination lock on its surface. I called out the combination as I spun it once left, once right and then left once more. I pulled opened the safe and showed Ebony my surprise. In front of her laid stacks and stacks of $100 dollar bills all wrapped in rubber bands.

"Oh my god Harlem!" she said in shock, "What is all this?"

"This is ours! I have been saving every penny I've made and keep some of it here."
I grabbed a stack of bills and handed it to her. She took the rubber band off and flipped through the bills.

"There's got to be millions of dollars here," she said in surprise.

"Yup and there's another 50 million in that safe," I informed her.
I closed the door and spun the combination in both directions. I closed the trap door and placed the boxes back where they were.

"I showed you this for one reason," I said looking Ebony in the eyes. "If anything happens to me or my family I trust that you'll know what to do with it."

VICTIM OF SUCCESS

QUINTIN

"Teach music to the child and you give the soul a voice." - unknown

Sometimes the real lesson was in the beat, sometimes the harmony, the point was there was always a lesson. Music had the ability to lighten moods, brighten souls and above all – teach a lesson. With only a handful of weeks left in the school year I could see the growth in my class. Their knowledge in musical instruments and musical genre's had expanded beyond what they watched on *106 and Park*. But growth in one area meant sacrifice in others. Nia and I started to grow distant since we returned from New York. Part of me felt it was because of the guilt I carried about kissing Spelling. Other parts wondered if she had found someone else or grew unhappy with my gambling. What made things worse is she had become distant and the permanent substitute teacher in her art class meant her return to work was null and void. I'd fallen into a deep depression; I'd lost my brother, my girl, so I turned to the one thing I had left – Dominos.

Intentions had a different vibe than normal nights. The club downstairs was packed. The NeoSoul ambiance was transformed into the epicenter of carnal desires. Tonight the Brothers of Nu Beta Psi held their annual Chocolate Party and the heat radiating off the half naked bodies below gave the tables upstairs an unusual warmth. Dee was preoccupied with entertaining the ruckus youth downstairs that his usual spot behind the desk was now filled with a cute sister who radioed to him when a new buy-in had arrived.

"Can you let Dee know that Quintin is here," I yelled to the girl behind the counter trying to shout over the excitement going on downstairs.

"Who?"

"Quintin – Quintin Bennet"

I turned and looked at Harlem who guarded my buy-in and kept a close eye on his business downstairs. Tonight's buy-in was slightly higher than normal since tonight's game involved partners. I was never a fan of playing with partners for money unless I knew my partner, but with a $10,000 payout each, I couldn't turn a blind eye.

"Q, my main man!" Dee screamed excited and out of breath.

"Money making Harlem, in the building," he acknowledged.

Harlem leaned over the counter to give Dee dap and exchanged a large wad of cash without anyone ever noticing. My guess was it was for allowing his soldiers to conduct business in his establishment without the fear of law enforcement. Dee accepted the gesture with a nod while slipping the knot into his pocket and turning his attention back to me.

"Crazy night on both floors," he pointed out showing me the gambling floor was filled to capacity.

"I've got you on table six, some real lightweight competition," he urged "so it should be an easy payout."

This time Harlem handed Dee an envelope filled with 5K in bills. We watched as he flipped through the bills with his usual routine then opening the safe behind him to deposit the cash.

Code blue, code blue...

The announcement over his walkie-talkie changed his demeanor when he turned around.

"Gentlemen, if you will excuse me business calls," he gestured to the device.

"Best of luck tonight."

"You all right Q?" Harlem asked sensing my mood.

"I've got a lot on my mind recently."

"Well now is not the time to let that take over you, there's serious money on the line chief so focus on business first and we'll talk about things later."

Harlem was right. Now was not the time to let things between Spelling and I cloud my focus. The strangeness of Nia's whereabouts since we returned from NY, my brother's death. It was time to put the Bennet family skill to good use.

The sounds of cheering and laugher could be heard around the floor as the winners made it known who they were. I sat watching my dominos doing my best to read my partners body language. Ninety percent of this game was non-verbal and my partner was only giving me the unwanted ten percent. Dee was right, this table was easy money but even easy money had a way of slipping through your fingers. The game started slowly with each player carefully laying pieces down, everyone seemed to be playing defense which was common when this much money was on the line. Once each player only held two or three dominos, the complexity of the game changed considerably. My partner, who'd been playing mediocre up till now, seemed to be making all the wrong choices. He blocked my move twice and then locked me from making any moves in the final plays. Our opponents shouted in victory and I looked around for answers. He just got up shrugged his shoulders and left the table with a smirk. I sat there shocked, searching the pieces for where I went wrong. I looked up to see my partner kissing the sister I'd lost to a while back on the same table and it became apparent my loss was part of a set up.

***

Ring... Ring...

My house phone rang causing me to lose focus.

> "Mr. Bennet, good evening this is Brother Wholesale and I'm calling to request your presence at our invite only-interest meeting. If you're interested, thirty minutes...the basement of Douglas dorms."

His statement was followed by a dial tone. I hung up not sure if I wanted to get involved.

I walked into a tiny room with twenty brothers of Nu Beta Psi at a head table. Eleven nervous brothers sat directly in front of them looking like they were being judged for their sins.

> "Good evening Mr. Bennett, please have a seat," Brother Wholesale directed me.
> "We have called all of you here today because we the Brothers of Beta Si will be creating a line of young brothers for the Spring semester. How many we choose is completely up to you, take a good look at

the other gentlemen that are here with you tonight, they will become your best friends for the next few months during your pledging process. To become a pledge there are a few requirements, starting with your GPA. All of our members must maintain a cumulative GPA of a 2.5. Most importantly, you must be able to follow the instructions and requests of all the brothers up here on the panel with me. In the next few days it will be your responsibility to get to know us as you earn the right to become a brother of Beta Psi."

The atmosphere in the room resembled boot camp and we were all about to lose our civilian privileges.

"Now on to business," Brother Wholesale continued. "On your seats are envelopes with information you're required to memorize. Eat and sleep the information on those pages for it will be the only thing that will help you survive this journey. You are all required to have $500 dollars cash to me by midnight tomorrow along with a copy of your transcript from the registrar's office. I would like to thank all of you again for coming on such short notice, but I would advise you all to go home and get some sleep, you're going to need it. This meeting is extremely classified and will operate in secrecy moving forward."

Just as quick as the meeting started, it was over. The room was quiet as the weight of becoming a part of Nu Beta Psi Fraternity Incorporated was proposed.

***

The hum of Nia's engine startled me from my sleep. I'd grown accustomed to the sound of her keys jingling in the front door early in the morning, so I rolled over and tucked the covers further over my head. Staying out late to ride with her girls was something she did often since we came back from up North. Tonight was the night I'd get answers to a relationship that was growing more and more distant.

"How come we don't talk like we used to?"

"Quintin not now, I'm tired."

"Well we never hang out any more so when would be a better time?"

"Listen Q, things have been real crazy for me the last few weeks and I just need some time to get my mind right."

"What's that suppose to mean?"

"That means we're moving too fast and I just need some time to think."

"Keep it real Nia, what's really going on?"

"Do you remember when we were on the subway in N.Y. and we ran into that guy?"

I instantly knew who she was talking about when she uttered those words; his face was forever etched in my memory.

"I remember, you said he was nobody."

"Well I lied. He was my old boyfriend that I ran away from. They called him Ninja because of the 250R he rode. He was great then, introduced me to riding and showed me the world. That's until he hit me. So one day I ran, I ran far...far away. When we saw him that day on the subway it made my skin crawl because I could see the anger in his eyes. It's only a matter of time before he finds me again."

"Finds you, you don't have to worry about him," I responded doing my best to console her. "I'm here now and I won't let him hurt you."

"No!" she responded pushing me away.

"I can't do this anymore," she announced brushing a tear from her eye.

I watched as she quickly gathered a bag and filled it with her belongings. Anger and fear leaving me standing there speechless when a simple "let's talk about this" would suffice. She stood in the doorway looking me over for assurance but in that moment I remembered Spelling, thought about the possibilities of reconnecting with my best friend and watched as the door shut behind her.

STRANGE FRUIT

MARQUEL

"It's funny how you can blow a reputation in five minutes that took a lifetime to build." - unknown

It didn't take long for both the link and the truth about my job at Body Language to get back to Eva. She packed a suitcase and Darius and took off on a Greyhound back to Miami to stay with her parents. The wound was too fresh for her to listen to my rationale or my reasoning. I understood; she needed time, but it hurt most to lose my son. He was too young to understand, I gave him excuses like: his grandparents missed him and wanted to see him, mommy was going to take him on a mini-vacation while daddy finished up school. She took him crying and screaming for his daddy.

To make things worse, I was experiencing a horrible burning sensation when I went to the restroom. I'd sent in blood work and urine samples weeks ago for answers. I had a feeling something was wrong when I got the call to come into the doctor's office for my results. Usually you got a call notifying you that everything was all clear but the request for my presence could only mean that I was dying or flirting with it instead.

I sat in the sterile waiting room watching the seconds on the clock tick bye. I glanced around the room and tried to guess what the handful of patient's waiting in the room were here to see the doctor for. Their reasoning would not be nearly as stressful as my return for the results of my STD test. I found an anonymous testing center not too far from campus and took the test after this viral video mess. Ever since they pricked my skin and took that vial of blood, I've been extremely paranoid. I didn't tell anyone because I was concerned about how they would perceive me, but every itch and tingling sensation made me question my health.

"Mr. Howard!" That cute intern shouted from the door in the corner of the room.

"Follow me," she smiled and sashayed down a long hallway with me right on her heels.

I watched as her nurse uniform hugged her just right and I fought to keep the thoughts that got me here in the first place out of my head. She opened the door slightly and directed me in.

"Have a seat Mr. Howard, the doctor will be with you shortly."

We both eyed each other down before I obediently took a seat and waited. The seconds felt like hours. My throat got dry and my palms began to sweat as I could feel a panic attack coming from the anxiety.

"Mr. Howard, how are things going?"

"I was hoping you could tell me Doc, I haven't been able to sleep properly since I took the test."

The doctor cracked a quick smile and cut right to the chase.

"I'm sure you're aware of why we called you in today? I have some good news and some bad news."

Hearing this sent a ringing pain to my head and I suddenly felt dizzy.

"I'll start with the good news," he spoke up noticing that I was slipping into a hysterical state.

"Your AIDS test came back negative," he announced with certainty.

A smile slowly broke across my face as I shot up screaming.

"Thank you! Thank you Jesus!"

"Mr. Howard!" he summoned, bringing me back to reality and the fact that there was still bad news looming. I sat and listened as he continued.

"Your STD test however, came back positive."

"What does? I mean, how bad... what kind of STD?"

"You tested positive for *Chlamydia Trachomatis*, or better known as Chlamydia."

"What?" I slurred a few more words before the doctor helped me out.

"It is a sexually transmitted bacterial infection. To be honest Mr. Howard you have a mild case of Gonorrhea."

Those words shot needles through my crotch with the thought of some bacteria eating away at my insides.

"Is there a cure?" I mustered enough strength to ask.

"Consider yourself fortunate, you really dodged a bullet. It is curable, but it could have been much more serious and severe.

His comment instantly angered me because it wasn't my decision to have unprotected sex. I started to question if Karen did this knowingly.

The doctor jotted down a few more things and closed the folder.

"Mr. Howard, life is better lived above ground. Using protection doesn't make you less of a man; it makes you a smarter man."

He handed me a prescription and left the room.

***

The studio had a different vibe today than any other. I imagined it had something to do with the

Board of Directors visit in a few minutes. Everything from today's topics to today's call-in responses just didn't have the same B.A.S.I.K luster I was used to. Chaz was somewhere in the backroom changing our Dat tapes when the four elderly gentlemen entered the studio. They looked like Donald Trump money from the sharpness of their suits.

"Mr. Howard, pleasure to meet you. My name is Franz Preston, President of the LAHU Board of Directors. The other gentlemen joining me are Paris Young, Vice President of Student Affairs, Dean Albright the Dean of your College and Mr. Fisher, head of the FCC."

"Pleasure to meet you all."

"Remarkable job you young men have done here," Dean Albright stated, shaking Chaz's hand as he joined us.

"Would you gentlemen mind giving us a tour of your operations?" Mr. Fisher asked amazed at how two young students in such a small studio could garner so much radio attention.

The tour of our tiny studio was filled with small talk and questions about our daily routine. The four men watched in astonishment as Chaz and I accomplished daily what large, fully-staffed studios did in a week.

"We're going to cut to the chase gentlemen," Mr. Young explained. Your tremendous work has lured the attention of a large media chain who is interested in buying out our tiny station."

"This is a tremendous opportunity," President Preston jumped in. "This merger will provide a lucrative relationship between our school and our new business partners."

Chaz and I looked at each other with extreme excitement. The possibilities of getting new equipment and possibly a new studio was the big break we both hoped for.

"The only problem with our new merger," Dean Albright confessed, "This will be the final semester of B.A.S.I.K. radio. It is in our best interest that we take the image of this new station in a different direction."

FOUR TWENTY

HARLEM

"There is no new News, just old News happening to new people." - unknown

We all gathered one last time in my grandparent's garage. The local Drug Enforcement Agency began stronger efforts to clean up the city of Atlanta, so it was only a matter of time before they came knocking. Squeeze and Shaa' were the first to arrive followed by Allure, Messiah, Thought, 20/20, Felony and Cardinal. Everyone knew what tonight's meeting was about so I wasted no time getting down to business.

"Word on the streets is we're being watched," I opened, making most of them paranoid and sending eyes searching around the room.

"I was notified that Faze has become a bigger problem and is working with the Narc squad to bring us down."

"What do you suggest we do?" Felony asked.

"We shut things down piece-by-piece and disappear like nothing ever happened. I hope most of you listened when I advised you to start saving which should make disappearing a bit easier."

"Campus is going to start dying down in a few weeks," Shaa' spoke up. "That will make it easier for me."

"The Athletes are winding down their seasons, so that should slow down my sales," Messiah announced.

"I can see a slow pull out from me and my foot soldiers," Squeeze followed.

"So we will start there, a gradual pull out from our Athlete's, Frat's, Sororities and general student branches. Then we will move out of the West and Eastside."

Everyone agreed and just like that the meeting was concluded.

***

"Faze, nothing we've compiled over the past few months will stick!" Detective Soul screamed.

"We've infiltrated his operations in New York, L.A., and Miami but haven't been able to find anything that will stick in a court of law."

"I've given you everything I have; I can't even walk the streets anymore because half the dealers in the area have a bounty on my head."

"We've narrowed Mr. Best's operation down to six main distributors in the area and all of them seem to be untouchable."

"We need you to do us one more favor."

"You're all out of favors, I need you to do something for me before I even consider helping you."

Detective Soul took a seat exhausted and frustrated. His department had already burned most of their funds and manpower on what was quickly becoming a wild goose chase. The young man from nowhere continued to move large amounts of narcotics throughout his district without any restriction or penalties.

"Something like what?"

The grin that spread across Faze's face meant he had already concocted a scheme to hit Harlem hard and somehow benefit himself in the long run.

"First I need protection, money and a new start, somewhere far away from here."

Soul rocked back in his chair debating the weight of his request.

"I may be able to make that happen."

"If you can make that happen, then I can give you the key to his city, the Achilles heel to his life - her name is Ebony."

***

I'd already shut down half of my business and it was making a lot of steady consumers very angry. To make things worse Legacy was upset his steady flow of cash had suddenly hit a drought. This was a direct impact to his bottom line and would certainly lead to an unannounced visit. Logic urged me to move Ebony and I into a sizable three bedroom place further from campus to stay unpredictable. In twenty-two years, I'd never seen the inside of a bank; never opened a bank account, used an ATM card or created a four-digit pin. I thought once about investing in a safety deposit box, but quickly came to my senses after I realized a paper trail would follow curiosity back to me. On the other hand I'd never seen the inside of a jail cell. The blank walls, the ugly metal bars that accompanied you when no one else would. So I stood in the middle of two worlds; crime and extravagance. The ability to buy whatever, whenever without a second thought or total disregard for consequences was a major perk. That was until Ebony; her young twists had begun to get some length and she pulled them back with a rubber band to keep them out of her face. Her skinny jeans hugged her curves as she stood planted in some white/white Air Force Ones. She looked just as beautiful today as she did when we first met in the student organization office.

"How are you my Queen?"

"Good my King."

"I've got some good news and some bad news," she stated with a smile. "Which one do you want to hear first?"

"I'll take the good news first."

"Your grandparents just told me that your brother, Arius just got accepted to Morehouse."

A Morehouse Man... I thought. A big part of me wanted him to follow in my footsteps and attend Lincoln Harris, but I understood his need to go out and be an individual.

"That's awesome news; I've got to get him something."

"Already taken care of," she responded taking out a new Apple Laptop.

"See that's why I love you!"

"So what's the bad news?"

I watched as she put the laptop down and walked over to me, her steps careful and controlled as if trying not to break egg shells. She took a seat next to me and rested her head on my shoulder.

"I'm Pregnant."

THREE THE HARD WAY

CAESAR

"A wise young man says father teach me; A foolish young man wants to live life freaky." – KRS One

We'd spent the last four hours in a tiny North Carolina holding cell. It reeked of disappointment and shame, a scent that revived memories of my delinquent past. Life was much easier to live when it's carefree; the more notoriety I gained the less effort I put forth. Even when word got back to Coach about our run-in with the law, he quietly paid his media connections a small fortune to keep it off the evening news. It seemed the more celebrity I achieved the more un-earned benefits we were presented.

Today, I had a photo shoot for *SLAM* magazine, just one of a handful of media engagements I had to fulfill. The lights in the interview room were hotter than South Beach in the middle of summer. I got there early knowing that I still had plenty to do for the rest of the day. The woman conducting the interview insisted on flirting with me to pass the time with her smiles and winks but I just wanted to get this over with. Just then Tia Springs swooped in the room looking even better than she did at the track meet. It felt like all the air was sucked out the room and her simplicity made her even sexier. She wore short shorts that exposed her well-defined legs, some *Air Max 95's* and a shirt that hugged her like the many men who watched her run wanted to. She smiled at me and took the available seat next to me. Her perfume made me want to jump all over her right there, but I had to maintain composure. The interviewer, noticing all my attention now on Tia quickly excused herself.

"I'm going to go and freshen up before I start the interview," she said with an attitude.

I had my chance, Tia and I were alone and there was no telling when this opportunity was going to happen again. Now came that moment of manly decision once again, I could just sit and watch this beautiful woman right next to me, exchanging no verbal communication, or man-up and go holla - I froze up. I was speechless, I couldn't think of anything to say and for the first time in my life a woman intimidated me.

"So, it's nice to finally meet you," Tia said, breaking the silence.

"I'm a really big fan," she said extending her hand for a shake.

"I saw you do your thing a few weeks back when you ate our track team up," I responded shaking her hand.

She blushed and smiled happy to hear that I admired her work.

"I apologize for being late but I came directly from another interview so I hardly have time for myself," she said.

"I understand, trust me I understand," we both laughed.

And just like that we hit it off.

***

After Tia, I filed for divorce from the player game. She captivated me like the first time I watched Streetball - I was amazed. I got rid of recreational therapy with Sherri, Tanya Tuesdays and Trisha Thursdays. I even dismissed Dion and Aisha, my go to miracle workers. Tia and I became the Bonnie and Clyde of College sports. We both lived our lives through the lens of media television. Every move critiqued, blogged and re-tweeted for everyone to see. We found solitude in each other, bonded by our love for our sport.

We both lay naked on my bed; the mellow vocals of Alicia keys crooned as my paintbrush glided softly across her nipples. We only got to relax like this when she was in town so I cherished the little time we shared. Her muscles were tone, defined and her smooth skin made her body the perfect canvas. She giggled as my brush tickled spots on her body no paintbrush had ever seen before. She ran her fingers over my arms admiring my tattoos. I was content knowing that somehow the pain I inflicted with my tattoos was my sentence for every broken heart, every innocent woman I corrupted, my passion for over-priced footwear and vandalizing artwork.

The sound of my cell phone somewhere in my sheets interrupted our precious time.

"Caesar, I have some bad news," Coach Newton stated. "Big Butta is dead."

WHEN THE MUSICS GONE

QUINTIN

"When you come to the end of your rope, tie a knot and hang on." – Franklin D. Roosevelt

It was two in the morning when I got the call; tonight's pledge duty was to meet the rest of the brothers of Beta Psi at the city cemetery located on the outskirts of town. The instructions were to wear all black, and tell no one of our whereabouts. This call came after a string of calls all week, like the one I got from Brother Juss. He decided one night that he needed a cheeseburger and I was the only one who could get it. It was my responsibility to respect my big brothers wishes so I dragged my ass out of bed and drove to the nearest Mickey D's. To my surprise he didn't like pickles on his burger so I needed to get him a fresh one without the pickle flavor on it and a milkshake that was only sold on the other side of town. By the time I got through with Brotha' Juss' late night munchies, the sun was practically coming up. After a hectic week like that I was well prepared for tonight. I quickly got up, threw on my black Timb's, jeans, shirt and doo-rag.

Two other guys on-line with me were already waiting by the time I arrived. They were practically invisible as they stood in the dark. Of the nine other guys on line with us, Truman and Link were two cool ass dudes. These two were really down to earth. Unlike the others they weren't in this frat thing just to get pussy or popularity; they just wanted a chance at being a part of something special; the Black Elite.

"What's good, Sir's?"

"Chillin Q, why the hell are we here?" they both asked in unison.

"I'm clueless, but it couldn't be that bad," I said, causing us all to laugh.

The real joke was the truth behind that statement. The past three and a half weeks had been a living nightmare for the eleven brothers on line. On the spot pop quizzes, all kinds of late night meetings and some of the craziest request. Our daily tasks never ended and when we assumed they were, they found something new to learn. There was always something for us to do and there was always someone there to make sure we did it. The older bro's joked about how easy we had it now and how challenging this was going to be, but in comparison to the first three weeks, we couldn't see it getting any worse.

Just as we started to build, Big Brother Wholesale arrived with the eight other line members, and a handful of other big brothers, all dressed in black too.

"Gentlemen?" he nodded, pleased with our prompt arrival.

"Everyone follow me!" Big Brother Wholesale shouted.

All of my line brothers filed in order and we marched in a single file line deep into the cemetery. I wondered where we could be headed and worst yet, what we were going to do when we got there. The path was dark, the wall of trees made every direction look identical. The crackle of twigs and leaves beneath our feet sounded like a sandpaper symphony echoed by old oak trees and tombstones. After traveling for what seemed like a good fifteen minutes, Big Brother Wholesale raised his hand, signaling our arrival at our destination. We all gathered around waiting for further instructions.

"Welcome young pledges, we are standing in what we Brothers like to call, Alcatraz, the city's biggest cemetery, which spans the length of three football fields in length and width. We have brought you here to play a game called "Escape from Alcatraz."

The pledges turned and looked at each other with puzzled looks, this game seemed an easy task as they turned back in for the instructions.

"We are now standing on the opposite side of the cemetery, your objective is to successfully make it back to the entrance and our game is complete."

Something felt wrong, what did he mean by 'successfully' make it back. I watched as Brother Wholesale snapped his fingers twice and all the active brothers disappeared into the darkness of the cemetery.

"Now gentlemen, there is a bit of a twist, my brothers have just made your path to the front of the cemetery a hard one. They have hidden themselves in trees, holes and behind gravestones with nitrous powered paint guns. Their all black appearance will ensure that your awareness level will remain at a minimum and the visibility zero."

I turned to see if I could see any brothers off in the distance, but like Big Brother Wholesale said they had disappeared into the darkness of the night. The cold breeze that was beginning to blow was now bringing a thick blanket of fog, which was going to make this game a little harder.

"You will not be given any armor or helmets; you will not be given any directions back to the front. We have purposely walked you through the forest that surrounds this cemetery to throw off your sense of direction. To make this game a bit more exciting, the brothers and

I have decided to give you these," and Brother Wholesale disappeared into the dark for a few seconds. He returned with a duffel bag and began handing out bright white t-shirts.

"These shirts will help the brothers and I keep an eye on you as you make your way back to the front," Brother Wholesale laughed to himself as he finished the sentence. "Good luck gentlemen," he directed and disappeared into the night.

My line brothers and I gathered ourselves with all the instructions we were just given and tried to make sense of everything. While putting on our white t-shirts, one of the new guys on line spoke up.

"I know a thing or two about paint guns, and nitrous powered guns make the paint pellets hit with the force of a bullet from thirty yards. They can shoot with the repetition of a semi-auto hand gun."

This new bit of information was a bit surprising, and a few more line brothers began to mumble to themselves. I turned to Truman and Link to get their opinions on our situation.

"I don't like this Q," Link spoke up.

"Yea, these white shirts are going to make us stand out in this dark ass cemetery and make us sitting ducks for flying paintballs." They were right, this game was quickly turning into an unfair

challenge of manhunt, and the cemetery
was going to be our battlefield.
Just as I finished my thoughts, the quiet sound of
a whistle came from behind us. It sounded like
and arrow breaking wind searching for the bulls
eye.

"Arghh!" we heard one of the brother's
yell as he hit the floor, his white shirt now
covered with what looked like red paint.
We all ran to his side for comfort, "You all
right man?" we all shouted, he grabbed his
shoulder with the look of sheer pain and
said it burned like hell but he was going to
be all right. Just then two more whistling
sounds came through the trees. We could
hear the sound of the first layer of tree
bark shatter as a paint pellet slapped the
tree, the other pellet hitting the floor just
shy of where we gathered around our fallen
brother.
"Find cover!" another brother yelled
dodging another pellet that fell short of the
entire group. The constant whistle of
pellets breaking the wind was our only
warning, signaling that the big brothers
were tired of us doing too much
socializing. Everyone tried to find cover
behind trees gathering themselves before
entering the war zone. I looked out from
behind my tree at the cemetery, which
looked like an ocean of tombstones. Our

only protection from the flying pellets was the cover of thick fog coming in, and our ability to stay undetected.

"Listen!" I shouted out to the other line brothers who were hiding behind their own trees, "The only way we'll have a chance is if we stay low and split up, maybe into groups of two or three, it may be harder for them to pick us off that way!"

Our twelve-man team was now down to eleven as we set out into the cemetery. I got down on my hands and knees and crawled out to the first tombstone. I placed my back to the cold slab of cement and signaled for the rest of the line brothers to follow. The next one out was a freshmen we called Justice. You could see the fright in his body as he stepped out from behind his tree. He panicked in the dark and ran recklessly out into the graveyard.

"Keep low!" I yelled, as the sound of three whistles came out of nowhere. I watched his body fall and his screams of pain echoed through the cemetery. *What am I doing*, I thought to myself, *these fools are crazy*. Truman and Link followed me to the next row of tombstones and we lay there with our backs to the stone.

"We're staying with you Queens!" they both yelled. We crawled on our stomachs through the cold, damp graveyard. Ten, nine, eight... the sound of screams and the constant sound of whistling meant that line brothers were falling like flies. We were spread out across the cemetery now and the last thing on my mind was panicking. My main concern was not to get hit with one of those pellets that were raining from everywhere.

I could see the gates to the front of the cemetery a few yards ahead of me. I assumed that Link, Truman and I were the only three still left as the whistles became less frequent. I could hear the rustle of footsteps in the woods as the big brothers tried to get a better shot at the remaining recruits. We stumbled through the entrance of the cemetery and got up in celebration. We had made it as a team through this ordeal and we felt stronger now, like we accomplished something, we had beat the big brothers at their own game and we celebrated with high fives. A barrage of whistles came out of nowhere and hit all three of us. We all hit the floor and rolled in pain, it felt like I had been pierced with needles and the pain only got worse. The only sound I can remember hearing after that was a bullhorn as Big Brother Wholesale stood over us holding a flame that lit up most of the entrance. We all tried to get to our feet despite the pain and we could see the wounded line brothers trickling in to the front one by one.

When everyone made it back to the front Brother Wholesale spoke again:

"Thank you gentlemen for coming out. The brothers and I will contact you again with our next meeting time."
And just like that it was over; I turned to Link and Truman who were still in pain. We all nodded in success while all of our line brothers hobbled off into the darkness.

IVY LEAGUE

MARQUEL

"Failure is the tuition you pay for success." – Walter
Brunell

My focus was getting my family back. With only
a handful of weeks left in school and only one
broadcast of B.A.S.I.K. left I was going to have
to pull out all the stops.

"Where you been, boy!" the intimidating
sound of The Mayor questioned on the
other end of my line.

"I've been sick, Desire didn't tell you?"

"Don't try that, she hasn't heard from you
either."

"That's right, I told Denim. I thought he
would have mentioned it to you both."

"Cut the crap, your clients are asking for
you and we're not covering anymore!"

"Everything alright Marquel?" the
mesmerizing sound of Desire's voice

questioned snatching the phone from The Mayor.

This was obviously the "good cop/bad cop" routine they were running.

"Our clients are priority baby," she reminded. "Without them there is no me, there is no you and more importantly there's no money."

"Yea and we coming for our percentage regardless of how sick your little ass is!" The Mayor screamed, as I realized now I was on speaker phone.

"I'll be back tomorrow," I responded reluctantly knowing that Body Language was only drifting me further away from Eva and Darius.

"What's this I hear about a video?" Desire questioned shifting the tone of the conversation.

"It was nothing," I urged prepared for a lecture.

"Yea, it was nothing that was recorded here. We saw the video!"

I hung my head pissed at how far this problem had spread.

"Listen Marquel, I thought we talked about how manipulative some women can be, how did you get in a situation like that?"

I let her question resonate for a minute. Truthfully the drugs she slipped me put me into that situation, but the real question was how did I get here? How did the money, lies and deceit become so much of me that I could lose everything?

"I'll be back in the office tomorrow," I assured them and hung up not answering the question.

* * *

I stood outside my room as I did many times before waiting for my next client. I introduced myself and ushered her in exhausted from riding the emotional rollercoaster the past few months. I stood in front of my sink washing my hands in preparation.

"I'll be with you in one moment," I stated, realizing my client was unusually quiet.

"What can I help you with?" I asked, turning to face the badge of an undercover police agent.

With her hand placed to her mouth in a quiet motion, she walked to the door and locked it.

"Mr. Howard, this can go one of two ways, you can give me the answers I'm looking for or I can radio for backup and we can arrest everyone right now."

"I'll help, what do you need to know?"

"We've had surveillance on Body Language for some time now. We have good reason to believe that your boss Joy Wright, better known as Desire is running a male prostitution ring out of this store front."

I listened in shame, knowing that all good things eventually came to an end.

"We've targeted you because we believe you can provide us with the physical evidence we need to solidify this case."

"What kind of evidence are you looking for?"

"Bank statements, client appointment books or merchandise inventory logs, anything that we can use against her that will stick in court."

"I'll be honest with you. Desire's guard dog, The Mayor keeps a watchful eye on all those things. You're better off trying him."

"Mr. Howard, I don't think you understand. This is now a Federal case, we're not talking about a petty slap on the wrist or a misdemeanor. You and your co-workers are all conspirators and will serve time when we slam the hammer on this business. We're coming to you because you're young; your records show you have a wife and a kid. We are willing to cut a deal with the D.A. and reduce your sentence so you can walk across the stage with the rest of your classmates."

Her words echoed in my head as if she had screamed thorough a megaphone. I was being offered a second chance for bringing down the only place in my life that provided solitude. I couldn't remember the last time I'd talked to Caesar, Marquel or Harlem so it was time I got my priorities back in order. It was time to get my family back.

"I'll do it, when will you need all this information?"

"You have 48 hours," she stated getting up and heading for the door.

"I wouldn't leave so soon if I were you, our sessions are usually 60 minutes and leaving so soon may raise a few eyebrows."

"You're that good?" she smiled and took a seat next to me. "I guess your reputation does precede you."

All of Body Language's important paperwork was inside of Desire's home office. I'd only been there once for my orientation but I could vividly remember where they were kept. Getting into her crib would be easy but getting into her office would be more difficult, I thought as I sat on her sofa. She was excited that I'd decided to stop by for some more hands-on training so she pranced around in the tightest outfit she could find. I watched as she continued to fill my glass to numb me up for seduction. What she didn't realize was college parties quickly taught me how to hold my liquor much better. I sometimes felt like Desire enjoyed seducing younger men. She was approaching her mid-thirties so being twenty-four empowered her approaching cougar-hood.

Ding Dong....

The sound of her doorbell ruined our session. We both looked at each other with confusion; she quickly looked for something to cover herself up with before answering the door. Her shock matched mine when we watched The Mayor walk into her foyer.
    "Mayor!"
    "Wsup girl, damn you're looking good, where you expecting me?"
His moment in the sun was ruined when he spotted me on the couch.
    "What's this little nigga doing here?"
    "We're just chillin Mayor, nothing to get worked up over."
    "Chilling huh, why is he chillin here?"
    "Come on in and stop acting a fool."
I could hear his grunt of annoyance as he walked in and took a seat. My window of opportunity was quickly closing so I improvised.
    "Can I use your restroom?"
    "Sure thing, it's down the hallway to the right."
I got up knowing exactly where the restroom was, two doors from her office and right where I needed to be. I got up leaving them in a heated conversation about nothing. I slammed the

bathroom door for effect and crept into her office. It was different now, much cleaner and better organized. No more papers scattered around the desk or manila folders stacked in the corner. Desire had become smarter about her business dealings and finances that information was no longer laying out for wandering eyes. I sifted through her desk looking for anything with numbers or figures I could use. Before I could find anything, I could hear Desire and the Mayor making their way to her office. I scrambled to find somewhere to hide as they entered.

"We aren't bringing in nearly as many clients as we were a few months ago," The Mayor coached. "We need to do something to help maximize our exposure."

"We can't afford to jeopardize the entire business for more sales. What we're doing is working so let's just keep it that way."

"My crown jewel, Young Denzel is single handedly bringing in more clients than we've ever had."

Desire gloated as she walked to her bookshelf and slid a stack of books to the side to unveil a small safe.

"Well I don't like that little nigga."

"Shut up, you're just mad because he's bringing in more money than you."

She opened the safe and pulled out what I'd been looking for - paperwork and a stack of bills sliding them to The Mayor.

"This should cover our overhead for the month."

They both headed out of the office still in their heated conversation. I quickly grabbed a stack of papers still hanging out of the safe. Just like that I'd begun to dismantle Desire, the Mayor and Body Language.

***

"Life is about constant progression. We spend our entire childhood being taught the valued importance of education. As you mature the significance of getting good grades becomes vital for acceptance into a good college. Completion of a good college is a necessity for achieving a good career; while a good career is equivalent to financial stability. Without this untaught progression of life most of your existence is spent on the outside looking in trying to figure out where you went wrong, why life dealt you a bad hand. Although there is no guaranteed success, the formula at least moved you to the front of the line during employment time. The reality of being a student here at Lincoln Harris is that only 26% of us actually graduated from High School. Only 17% of us would toss our caps in the air come commencement. Of the 38.7 million black people in the U.S. the median family income of $33,000 vs. the $35,000 price tag for higher education eclipses reality. These staggering numbers are constantly disregarded as we stumbled from after party to after party. These figures are repeatedly ignored as we strolled into lectures late, cram at the last minute for exams or neglected to turn in lab assignments. Twice as many black women attended college than men, but instead of that being a motive to pull more brothers into the folds of knowledge, we foolishly turn our attention to the endless variety of fish in the sea and continue the deterioration of valuable black relationships. Let's face it, the stars that were once unreachable are now right at our finger tips so let's not let this opportunity of advancement we've earned slip away."

I quietly took my headphones off and rocked back in my chair exhausted. I could see Chaz in the other room punching buttons with the look of shock and amazement on his face. This was the final broadcast of B.A.S.I.K. radio and I could sense a little piece of me vanishing with the closing show. It all felt pointless, precious seconds of my life I could never get back.

GARGAMEL

HARLEM

"To eat an egg, you must break the shell." - Jamaican Proverb

I was surprised it had taken so long but I quietly sat across the table from Dr. Bird and Legacy who flew in and demanded my attendance. Dr. Bird who was once young in spirit was now aged and feeble requiring a cane to support his lanky frame. While the Empire insisted they accompany me, I demanded I come alone to finish what began decades ago. Network and Mandatory still guarded Legacy who appeared to walk with Dr. Bird out of kindness or request – I couldn't tell.

"Times have changed," Dr. Bird proclaimed. His voice was raspy and hoarse.

"Legacy tell mi yuh dun with our arrangement?"

"Dr. Bird, I am no longer Little Dread that moved bricks in a backpack to the docks years ago."

"Yea but wha mek you tink you can just gwan so? Wi have a business to run!" Legacy chimed in.

"You may own the product, you may run our tiny island back home, but you don't own me." I reminded him.

Dr. Bird held up his hand signaling our emotions were already boiling too hot.

"So much of you reminds me of uno Little Dread," Dr. Bird continued. "Just like you I born and grow inna di business from a yute. But mi neva had the opportunities you have."

He said looking around the room in amazement.

"Eighty percent!" Legacy reminded both of us. "Wi come fi collect."

"Collect wha?" I responded, now frustrated.

"Calm unu self," Dr. Bird reminded sounding more like the man I met years ago.

"This will be the end of it."

"Pure sufferation fi wi," Legacy mumbled under his breath.

"It's time you get off your ass and mek wi some money Legacy!"

I sat there shocked. I watched as Network and Mandatory rushed to assist Dr. Bird from his seat.

"Do me a favor Little Dread,"

"Anything."

"Learn everything, not many youth from our island get to leave much less get an opportunity like yours."

"Yes sir,"

Legacy followed them out the room flashing me his gun finger gesture on his way out.

***

Ebony had left hours ago for class and it wasn't like her to stay out all hours of the night. I sat worried in our apartment as a Heineken and the telephone accompanied me. Like clockwork I called her cell phone every hour on the hour hoping to hear something. The phone finally rang and I picked it up before it could finish the first ring.

"Ebony!"

"Listen here, if you want to see your girl alive again we want $2 million by 8:00 pm. tomorrow.

"Who is this?" I asked in desperation.

"This is your worst nightmare so don't fuck with us."

"We'll call you back in 30 minutes with more information."

That statement was followed by a dial tone. It could have been anyone; I'd built up such a large pool of enemies in the past few months there was no telling who could have taken her. I hung up the phone in a panic realizing it wasn't just

Ebony they had taken. There wasn't any amount of wealth or popularity that was worth losing their lives. I picked back up the phone and called the Empire for support.

Allure was the first one to arrive since the two of them had become extremely close.

"What are we going to do? She asked in a panic.

"What do you mean I'm going to give them what they want? I can't lose her, not now."

The phone rang again and we both grew silent.

It was time to get the rest of the instructions...

It was time to rescue Ebony.

The entire Empire arrived at the Georgia Aquarium the next day. A tiny area just outside of the Coldwater Quest exhibit was the exchange point for Ebony and a smart idea by the kidnappers to avoid any public retaliation. Our instructions were to bring two-million dollars in cash and four-pounds of our best product to the exhibit at one-o'clock. Their request was insignificant in comparison to Ebony's safety and the lack of sleep the past 24-hours confirmed that. The drugs and money were both smuggled in through a side entrance and placed in a garbage can, which we all surrounded. The Aquarium was filled to capacity and almost impossible to single out one person from another. We all stood searching the crown for our next step. I faintly spotted Ebony fighting her way through the crowd towards me.

"Ebony!" I shouted running to her.

"Are you o.k.? are you hurt? Did they touch you?"

"Girl we are so glad to see you," Allure sighed.

In that moment we all felt safe.

"The whole thing was a setup," Ebony responded.

Felony, a man about his money rushed to the garbage can and knocked the lid off.

"The money and the product are gone."

"How?"

"It was sitting over a trap door so they must have taken it when we weren't looking."

We all turned to Ebony for answers.

"It was Faze and his boys, their working with the cops. This place is crawling with D.E.A. They needed to get all of you together in one place so they could identify you all.

Awaiting the worst, we all gazed around suspicious of everyone.

"Let's get out of here," Ebony stated. "If they haven't arrested us yet then we still have some time."

Just like that, we huddled together and headed for the exit.

***

I had about an hour left before I had to be at Regency for the fair and I stood in the mirror tying the perfect knot on my tie. My suit was pressed and I was ready to impress the judges with my new strain. I was excited about today and the feeling of positive change was in the air. I had my portfolio laid out, my shoes nice and shined and I was tying my dreads back in the bathroom when the sound of my front door breaking in startled me. Before I could react my apartment was filled with cops dressed in black with their guns drawn and screaming.

"Get down on the floor right now... right now!"

"Don't move... don't move!"

I was pushed to the floor and my face lay firm against the tile on the bathroom floor. I could hear Ebony screaming in the background as police ran from room to room giving the all-clear call. I could feel the slap of cold handcuffs on my wrist as I was brought to my feet.

I was turned to face an ol' school looking detective who wore a bulletproof vest under his sharp brown suit.

"Mr. Best, you are under arrest, you have the right to remain silent, anything you say can and will...." The rest of his rhetoric was lost as I was ushered to the back of the squad car in a daze.

BLACK FRIDAY

CAESAR

"Basketball doesn't build character. It reveals it." - unknown

The opening rounds of the tournament were a breeze when compared to the media frenzy that followed. I had a harder time answering the repetitive questions about the death of Butta during pre-game interviews. Tennessee, our first round opponents, were walk over's, followed by Duke and Arizona in the second and third rounds. Florida was the only team standing between us and another championship. They were known for their hustle play, quick guards and aggressive big men. L.A.H.U was still a five-point favorite and every major news and sports channel would be there to broadcast it. I sat in the locker room exhausted after our final practice for the season. The T.V. in the locker room was on *ESPN* and Stuart Scott was premiering "Inside the Coliseum," the all-access behind the scenes look at our team's season. A few of us had been here before, but the freshmen were nervous by the amount of attention being in the NCAA finals attracted.

"Gentlemen...Gentlemen!" Coach shouted, obviously excited about the upcoming game. We've had a season filled with ups and downs. While we continue to mourn the loss of our brother we can't forget why we're here. We are right where we need to be, we've earned the right to be in the finals and you've proven that with your game play throughout the season. I don't know a better way to thank you all for a spectacular season. You can all reward yourselves by finishing what you started. You have an opportunity to do something that no other University has done and that alone should be the only encouragement you need. So when you hit that court in a few days, don't play for L.A.H.U, don't play for me, the alumni or stats, play for your honor, your respect, and your future."

Just like that coach exited and went to join the rest of the coaches in the other room. The room grew silent with unease, before I decided to step up and say something.

"Look guys, now's the time! We've worked hard all season and became a family when critics said it couldn't be done. Playing ball is what we've been doing all season so let's not stop now. We need to do this for Big Butta"

I had everyone's attention in the room as all these emotions from my past flooded me; the issues with my father, supporting my moms, Tia, the media and Patten. I could hear my voice start to tremble and my eyes began to water. Before I knew it I was having an emotional breakdown right in front of the entire team. What I thought they would view as a sign of weakness actually fueled them as they all gathered around me for support.

> "We're with you, Caesar, we're honored to have you as our captain and we all realize we wouldn't be here if it wasn't for you." One of the younger players said, while the rest of the team agreed in unison.
> "Caesar on three...! Caesar on three...!" another freshman yelled.
> "1...2...3...Caesar!"

I was suddenly filled with pride and honor to know that my team was behind me. Everyone perked up after that and the locker room was filled with high hopes and energy. The coaches hearing the buzz and commotion came out from the other room and smiled seeing the energy in the room. Coach could see the emotion in my face and nodded his head. It was his way of saying job well done; I finally understood what it meant to be a leader.

***

The sound of the familiar engine roared as I lay blind folded in the back seat. The secure knots placed on the ropes around my wrists and ankles mixed with the cars high speed caused my large frame to bounce around in the spacious cockpit. I'd just gotten off the bus when I was hooded and abducted. I was sure it was some jealous boyfriend looking for revenge, or some nut job looking for a ransom handout. My only hope was my absence would cause alarm, so I kept my mouth shut and hoped for the best.

The bright light caused me to squint until my pupils adjusted to the light. The three brothers surrounding me bared no resemblance and the abandoned factory shared no familiarity. We waited in silence for hours until the doors to the factory swung open. I looked up just in time to see Charles Patten swagger in followed by his familiar bodyguard.

"Mr. Gibson, how nice of us to meet again, I am terribly sorry that it had to be under these circumstances but you are a very hard man to get a hold of."

"I was coming to see you, Mr. Patten I swear."

"Sure Mr. Gibson," he responded snapping his fingers twice.

His entourage disappeared into the dark leaving the two of us to work out the details.

"I wanted to thank you for that loss a few months back."

"Listen I've got your money back at the spot, I'm not interested in throwing games."

"That's where you're wrong; my offer is no longer an option Mr. Gibson. All of this national attention you've earned has now made this deal non-negotiable. I need you to lose the championship game in a few weeks."

"Look Mr. Patten, I don't want to complicate things. Untie me and I'll be happy to give you back your briefcase, then we can go our separate ways."

"How high in the draft would Atlanta's star athlete go with a broken arm? Or maybe a broken leg?" he laughed.

His laugh was strangely convincing. I struggled to wiggle out of the ropes in desperation. One of Patten's goons stood over me with a large metallic pipe in his hand while I could feel the second one standing at attention behind me.

"Look Mr. Gibson, a loss is all that's required; you've done it once so one more loss is insignificant."

This was the first situation my good looks couldn't rescue me from, the first circumstance that our boosters couldn't bail me out of. Neither my six-foot frame nor my jump shot could undo this mess.

"We're not going to lose..."

Those were the last words I remember saying before the cold feeling of that metal pipe swiped the back of my head.

AND THE BEAT GOES ON

QUINTIN

Music is what feelings sound like.

My house phone startled me from my sleep. I did my best not to wake Spelling who lay asleep next to me. Spelling and I grew closer as Nia and I grew further apart. Her weekend visits turned into week long sleep over's and in theory I'd finally got my best friend back.

> "Yo Q, this is Brother Wholesale, we're having a meeting in 30 minutes," he said, followed by a dial tone.

Damn, I thought to myself, *these guys have the worst timing*. I got up and snuck out the apartment leaving Spelling fast asleep.

When I arrived at the frat house the twelve brothers that started on line had been cut down to seven.

> "My brothers... My brothers... we have gathered here tonight because you seven gentlemen are one step closer to pledging."

Good, I thought because I was getting tired of these late night rendezvous.

"Your last test and challenge before crossing will be to test your will power," *What the hell was he talking about?* I thought.

"Tonight we begin, two weeks of seclusion. You are to have no contact with anyone for the next ten days, not your mother, your father or your friends, to assure this you all will live here in our house and only leave to attend class and exams."

I couldn't believe what I was hearing. I hadn't seen my true friends in months so there was no way in hell I could do this. I got up from my seat and headed for the front door.

"Mr. Bennet, may I ask where you're going?" Brother Wholesale asked motioning for the two brothers at the door to block my path.

"This isn't the type of brotherhood I had in mind," I told him turning to see his reaction.

"Are we asking too much from you Mr. Bennet? Is two weeks of your time too much to ask, for a lifetime of brotherhood?"

I thought about his question for a moment...

In the past few months I'd lost my brother, I let the only woman I loved walk out the door and gambled away my tuition in intentions. I was out of control, I was no good to no one like this. I pushed my way past the two brothers guarding the door and never looked back.

**

I needed to get away so I headed to the only oasis I had left, *Intentions*. With whatever money I could gather up I walked blindly like the night my brother died. My emotions felt like twelve rounds between love and hate and even the score card ended up even. Dee found me at the Black Jack table lost and looking for answers in the cards.

"The phone is for you," he said handing it to me.

His face was filled with fear and confusion.

"Yo!" I answered frustrated.

"Quintin honey?" my mother's voice said softly breaking me out of my slump.

"Something happened to Nia, and I need you to sit down."

My mother and Nia had become real good friends these last few months; they'd grown even closer since the death of my brother.

"What's wrong with Nia, Mom?" I shouted.

"Calm down, calm down" she demanded as Dee rested his arm on my shoulder.

"There was an accident, Nia was hurt, we don't know how bad but she's in the hospital."

My mother's words echoed in my ears over and over, "which hospital?", "When did this happen?" I dropped the phone and walked to the exit numb and stunned. I could hear Dee telling the dealer to close out my hand and could feel his glare on my back.

I was right by her side by the time my parents got there. The doctor said she was blind-sided by a driver and was knocked un-conscious. She had been out for a few hours and the doctor said she was lucky to walk away without any broken bones or limbs. I was just happy that she was still with me. I'm glad my parents came to support me, we were all getting very attached to Nia and they felt like it was one of their kids laying there in that bed.

"Quintin, honey, why don't you come back to the hotel with us and get some sleep?" my mother asked.

"Yea son, you need some rest," my father instigated resting his hand on my shoulder. Although I hadn't seen him since Quincy's funeral, it was still good to have his support.

"I would like to be here when she wakes up," I told them both and they understood. They gathered their things and left me alone to be by her side.

The beeping sound from her heart monitor chimed like a hammer beating on my temples. Nia had been out for hours and it felt more like an eternity. I squeezed her hand and prayed for the best. Ever since the first day we met the two of us were inseparable. For the first time in my life something meant more to me than music, more than Dominos or my fitted hats. I felt a moment of helplessness in my life, there was nothing I could do to help her.

"Quintin, is that you?" Nia asked opening her eyes for the first time.

"What happened? Where am I?" she said surveying the room for answers.

I felt a huge relief at that moment and my eyes began to fill with tears.

"You're in the hospital, baby. You had an accident on your bike."

Before I could finish my sentence two officers entered the room and stood in silence.

"We're sorry to interrupt," one officer announced.

"We just have a few questions to ask so we can finalize our paperwork."

"The car that hit you, we found it a few yards away from the scene of the accident totaled. The driver of that vehicle was killed instantly."

Nia, who was still squeezing my hand, squeezed harder as if the officers news was a victory.

"Can you tell us anything about the car or the driver?"

"It all happened so fast, I didn't get a good look at the car or the driver, sorry."

The officers looked at each other, apologized for the interruption and quietly left the room.

"It was Ninja, he was the driver," She whispered as a smile glided across her face.

"I told you he'd find me. He pulled up next to me that night at a red light. I panicked and took off and he followed."

Her situation of grief had suddenly become a lifetime of relief.

"We were going so fast, he clipped my back tire, his car slammed into a pole and went up in flames."

She laid her head back down and sighed, "You always said that thing was a death trap," she said making us both break out in laughter.

"I'm glad you're here," she turned squeezing my hand.

"I'm never leaving your side again."

"Put your future in good hands - your own."

EPILOGUE

MARQUEL HOWARD

Tomorrow's Activist

"It is better to be a failure at something you love than to be a success at something you hate." – George Burns

The sound of bullhorns and spontaneous screams filled the large auditorium of Lincoln Harris. The sea of students draped in black robes filled every available seat around me, while the robotic sound of names being announced broke my blank stare. I sat scanning the crowd for my family who sat proudly that their son had finally made it. After all we'd been through Eva, her family and my son Darius were all there. It was going to take some work but Eva was willing to take me back. I was willing to work as hard as it took for my family, for the sake of our marriage and for the sake of our love.

National news picked up coverage of the Atlanta Police infiltrating Body Language and pictures of Desire and the Mayor were on every channel. Both were charged with embezzlement, money laundering and a long list of other charges. Their sentence was extended for their involvement in the prostitution ring. I worked a plea deal with the judge to help Zae' and Denim, although their funds were frozen they never really saw any jail time and walked away with a few months community service. B.A.S.I.K radio was eventually bought out by that major network and both Chaz and I were replaced with new on-air personalities. Our departure eventually caused listeners across the country to change the dials and B.A.S.I.K slowly faded into the background.

I decided to use my vision of activism to ink a deal with a television station that depicted only positive aspects of African Americans in society. It was my opportunity to ensure we wouldn't go down in history as the generation lacking morals and family values. At least the youths of tomorrow could unplug from the Matrix and learn something other than who would win the next Music Award.

CAESAR GIBSON

Signing Day

"Sometimes, you find yourself in the middle of nowhere, and sometimes, in the middle of nowhere, you find yourself." - unknown

It was coach's suspicion about Charles Patten that saved my life that night. He showed up with the cops to find my body still bound to the chair and my leg broken in three places. Patten was able to get away, but the media had a field day once Coach leaked that he'd been secretly paying college athletes to manipulate scores for years. Patten was eventually sent to prison along with my secret of his bribe money. My leg healed over time but I was never the same. I lost the ability to cut and slash like I could before the injury. I could no longer explode off that leg for rebounds, jump shots and the physical play needed to compete at the next level. I fell from projected number one draft pick in that year's draft to not being drafted at all. I played a few years overseas and for a handful of teams in the D-League but my dreams of playing in the pros never came true. Lincoln Harris went on to win its third straight championship without me, etching our school in college basketball history. I auctioned off multiple pairs of my deadstock sneakers and donated all the proceeds to Big Butta's family in memory of my basketball brother. The media eventually stopped covering me, my endorsement deals faded and I became a memory.

Coach Newton eventually retired as Head Coach for Lincoln Harris University and destiny returned me right back to the same office, behind the same desk, sitting in that big leather chair. Behind me, hung trophies, plaques and newspaper clippings of my unbelievable basketball career. Stacks of playbooks and new offenses were scattered all over my desk as I pointed to the seat on the other side.

"Did you ever play in the NBA Coach?" questioned our new Freshman recruit.

I sat back in my chair and smiled at the irony in his question while wearing those exclusive *Air Yeezy's* on my feet.

QUINTIN BENNET

A New Beginning

"In the end we only regret the chances we didn't take, relationships we were afraid to have, and the decisions we waited too long to make." - unknown

I stood patiently on the steps of the hospital awaiting Nia. When you're faced with a life and death situation, things you took for granted meant more than ever. I watched nervously as they wheeled her through the front doors of the hospital where I waited.

"Hey baby?" she shouted getting up from the wheelchair slowly.

We all surrounded her for support scared of her frailty.

"I'm o.k. everyone," Nia announced.

The comfort of her voice made us all laugh at each other for our overreaction. Our smiles and hugs quickly grew silent as I cleared my throat giving everyone the cue.

"Nia, I have something important I want to ask you."

"My life has been really hectic the last couple of months and I feel it was you who helped me stay grounded despite all the craziness going on. You and my family have become really close and they love you like you were one of their own. I wanted to do this ever since your accident but I wanted everything to be perfect for you." I said reaching into my pocket and grabbing the tiny box that held our future.

I dropped to one knee and all the attention in front of the hospital was drawn to me. Nia instantly knew what was going on and she began to fluster with excitement.

"Nia Jones will you do me the pleasure of being my wife?"

Her eyes filled with tears as she screamed *"yes"* with reassurance in her voice. I quickly got to my feet and hugged her to join in the happiness. Everyone broke out into applause and cheered as I held my fiancé and my future in my arms.

EBONY

Trojan Horse

"Some people feel the rain. Others just get wet." –
Bob Marley

I sat on the other side of the visitation glass
twirling my locks nervous in anticipation. Time
and experience gave them the length of Harlem's
and the cowrie shell that hung from my loc'
symbolized my love for this man. Our child, still
growing within me, kicked and squirmed as we
waited for Harlem to join us. Being held with no
bond made all the money he accumulated
irrelevant and the bad news I was here to deliver
was making my throat tight and uncomfortable to
swallow. I perked up once I saw Harlem walk in
being escorted by a guard. I forced a smile and
picked up the phone.

      "Hey Empress, look at that stomach," he
reminded me.

"How are you, are they treating you ok?"

"I'm fine," he assured me placing his hand on the glass as if trying to caress my face.

"Believe it or not, I made a lot of these guys rich with my product so I'm respected by many."

"Good," I mustered the strength to say.

"What's wrong?"

I hung my head low in shame and looked up with tears in my eyes.

"The money is gone."

"What are you talking about?" he asked confused.

"It's all gone! For months I've shuffled your money between off shore accounts under different names. I created mock businesses and funneled your old bills back into circulation to eliminate tracing them back to me."

"What are you talking about Ebony?" he sat back in his chair trying to make sense of my confession.

"Once our place was raided, I went to your Grandparent's garage and filled two bags with money. A third bag I filled and gave half to your grandparents and the other half to your brother Arius."

"What did you do with the other two bags?"

"I gave them to my brother," I answered ashamed because he was catching on to my betrayal.

"Your who?" he questioned.

I could feel his anger mounting between the partition glass between us. The level of betrayal was so deep I didn't know where to start. It was my brother who encouraged me to be the Empire's Liaison for *Tropics*. He wanted me to keep an eye on Harlem and said he would let me know when he needed my help. I had no intentions of falling in love with him or becoming so entwined in this underground world. The school year was almost over until I received the call I feared. He needed all the information I'd acquired, the names and players of The Empire. The rotation and location of his grow houses. I had no idea what he wanted with it or his obsession with Harlem.

"Who is your brother?" he questioned.

I'd never seen Harlem angry, in the months that we'd become close he was always a caring and loving man who avoided conflict and drama at all cost.

"His name is Legacy."

ACKNOWLEDGMENTS

I would first like to thank God for blessing me with this gift to communicate through words. Without him none of this would be possible.

All of life's experiences contribute to making us who we are; who we become is credited to our journey through hardship and our ability to endure those times.

College for most of us is a time of personal growth and experiences that will be remembered forever. For me, college was a time of up's and down's and an opportunity to sharpen my skills as a writer. Thanks to everyone who contributed in making me who I am today. My Mother and Father, thanks for being the light that always guided me in the right direction. My baby sister, thanks for being an inspirational spirit that always kept me smiling when times got bad. My wife, who always encouraged me to work on my book even when I didn't feel like it would make much difference. My Son and Daughter, you are the future I envisioned for myself. I hope one day when you're old enough to read this you can be proud of your father and humor yourselves when you're finished with college. To my boys, Anthony Jumpp (XtraP), Jason Rose (Jayroctomologist), Shaun Johnson (B.D.I), Sa'Quhan Hollis (Hollywood), Robert Graham (R.G.), Derek Teasley (DTease), Clint Servantes (Sik Intellect) and Vince Balsamo (Balsami) thanks for the fellowship, you're crazy enough to be my friends so I'm crazy enough to give you a shout out. To my countless Cousins, Aunts, Uncles and other associates, you are all the backbone of a young writer trying to make a small dent in this big world.

Thanks to the five elements of Hip Hop, Caribbean culture, the Sneakerhead community and the sport of basketball. My love for each of you attributed to shaping both me and the characters in this book.

Finally, you the reader. Thank you for picking up this book, for taking time out of your life to read it and for letting me into your hearts, minds and imagination.

I hope that one day this project evolves from these pages into something much greater. May the wisdom in this book one day inspire the next generation of college goers and thinkers to achieve their own level of greatness.

Aquanza

Go to college, it's the only place you can truly find yourself.